T0149414

Also by Janice Mau

SAMOVARS AND SHASHLIK
Gems of an Overseas Adventure

UNSEEN SONGS

Janice Mau

BALBOA.
PRESS
A DIVISION OF HAY HOUSE

Balboa Press books may be ordered through booksellers or by contacting:

Balboa Press
A Division of Hay House
1663 Liberty Drive
Bloomington, IN 47403
www.balboapress.com.au
1 (877) 407-4847

Print information available on the last page.

ISBN: 978-1-5043-0730-7 (sc)
ISBN: 978-1-5043-0731-4 (e)

Balboa Press rev. date: 03/29/2017

For my sisters, God's daughters.
You never fail to encourage and inspire me.

Praise for
UNSEEN SONGS

"Jan's stories are easy to read and well written. Highly enjoyable for those days when a book is all that's needed."
Nascosta Incristo
Author
For This Cause, Against All Odds.

"An entertaining story that will warm you and leave you wanting more. I thoroughly enjoyed reading this book."
Jo Repo
Photographic Restoration and Design.

"An unforgettable read, highly engaging, and full of intrigue. Containing many hidden gems of wisdom and guidance, it is amazingly relevant. Although set in a fictional story, the truths contained within are life changing. I highly recommend this book for every reader."
Anita Greening
Co-Senior Pastor
Vineyard Christian Church

"I do not remember a beginning.
I walk the Earth; I dance through the heavens.
I sing to the many; I sing to the few.
I reveal myself to whomsoever I choose."

Book I

Weeping may endure for a night, but
joy cometh in the morning.[1]

The eagle glides across the steep slopes of the high escarpment, its wings glowing silver in the moonlight. The great bird's attention has been caught by a sound—the sound of someone singing.

The eagle swoops down on mighty wings and comes to rest on a rocky crag close to the source—a tall figure in a long flowing cloak—a cloak of shifting lights and shadows.

The majestic bird dips its head. The eagle knows who the singer is, for the knowledge is woven into its DNA as it is with all creatures, even human ones. Listening to the beautiful song, the great bird knows that Change is coming.

The One who is singing, gazes down, seeing the cloying darkness in the little community below.

The Founder implemented this darkness; nurturing and nourishing it long ago.

The Founder—a man who denied his followers freedom, bound them in chains of oppressive legality and refused them the most fundamental right of all—the right to have a name.

The singer's face sets in grim determination. He is going to break those soul-destroying chains, and turn the people's lives upside down, in a way none of them can imagine!

CHAPTER 1

A Foolish Decision

"What am I doing? Am I a fool?"

The Teacher paces backward and forwards, his eyes nervously darting between desk and door. He is sweating, and his hands are clammy. How can he have let it come to this? *My dratted temper. That's how!*

The morning had started off like any other. His son had been getting ready for school, and his wife had gone to collect water from the village water pump.

He had been searching for some misplaced pieces of parchment. Nothing important. Just some notations he'd made a few weeks back.

He'd looked in the pantry cupboard when he'd failed to find the parchments anywhere else. Although why he'd thought the parchments would be in there, was anybody's guess. As he had peered inside the cupboard, his feet had kicked against the wooden vegetable box, causing it to rock slightly. He'd knelt down, wondering why the box was sitting unevenly. When he'd picked the box up, he'd found a small package underneath. Wondering what it was, he'd opened it.

Hidden inside were his two pieces of parchment and something else.

Holding the discovery in his hands, he had agonized over what he should do. He'd decided to rewrap the package and return it to its hiding place.

He had found it difficult to focus on work, due to his stomach churning, and his thoughts vacillating between fear of what would happen if he reported the discovery and fear of what would happen if he didn't.

The last fear had won the tug of war, which is why he is now standing in the inner office of the Code Keeper, in the Great House.

He looks around the austere room from which all Code Keepers govern and control the people of the Code. It is sparsely furnished, with no warmth whatsoever. *Not unlike the Code Keeper himself.*

The Teacher exhales loudly through pursed lips.

His wife is the one who hid the forbidden items. There's no question about it.

The Teacher runs his hands through his hair in exasperation. *The dratted woman is like a hayseed up the nose.*

He wonders why she would do something so foolish, not to mention dangerous. The silly woman knows that breaches of the Code incur serious punishment or worse, depending on the depth of sin and the Code Keeper's frame of mind; a mind that can swing from mildly irritated to the fury of a raging bull in the space of a heartbeat.

How is the Code Keeper going to respond to his report?

Even worse, what punishment will he mete out?

The Teacher groans and kicks petulantly at a nearby chair. He should have ignored the items. That would have been the intelligent thing to do. He eyes the door, as panic takes over. Can he get out of the building before the Code Keeper arrives? *It's worth a try.*

He spins on his heel and strides quickly across the room. However, just as his hand reaches for the latch, the door opens.

CHAPTER 2

"Judas."

The Code Keeper steps into his office, bumping into the Teacher in the process. The Teacher has the look of a startled rabbit, and the Keeper frowns, wondering if the Teacher has just arrived or if he'd been attempting to leave.

Acknowledging the Teacher with a curt nod, the Code Keeper sits down behind the large desk on which there are parchments, beakers of quills and an old book.

The Keeper leans back in his chair and closes his eyes, pondering for a few moments, the tiresome vagaries of the people.

He'd have thought that the people would be shining examples of piety and godliness by now. However, they are not! Despite endless teaching, and applications of *Righteousness* (he touches the silver-handled horsewhip hanging from his belt,) they continue to be like silly sheep; needing a firm hand and a strong arm.

While the Code Keeper ruminates on the deficiencies of his Flock, the nervous Teacher stares at the Keeper's face, trying to gauge the Code Keeper's frame of mind. However, the closed narrow features aren't giving anything away.

The Code Keeper opens his eyes, catching the Teacher off guard.

The Keeper's bushy gray eyebrows plunge downward, and his features tighten in annoyance.

"What are you gawping at, man? Spit out your report! I've no time to waste on dithering fools."

The Teacher draws in a shaky breath and makes his report, words tumbling out in a nervous rush.

The Keeper listens without interrupting.

When the Teacher finishes his report, he waits for the Keeper's response.

A few seconds pass in silence.

The long pause induces a spark of hope in the Teacher. Hesitantly, he puts it to the Keeper that, seeing the items are small, couldn't his wife's foolishness be treated as a *minor* misdemeanor? One he can deal with at home?

The Keeper jerks forward, slamming the palms of his hands down on the desktop. His voice thunders.

"You know the law! You know the Code! It is your duty as men, to convey its teachings to your wives and children. If you had been teaching *your* wife correctly, she would not have sinned. I have no choice but to deal with her as *I* see fit."

The Keeper stands up and points to the door.

"Go back to work. The matter is no longer your concern."

The unfortunate Teacher stumbles from the room, his mind pointing an accusing finger: *"Judas."*

CHAPTER 3

"Piffle and nonsense."

High in the mountains, beams of sunlight shine down, piercing the dark gloom of the ancient forest. A tall, cloaked shadow passes through the narrow bands of light-shadow-light. Booted feet make no sound on the rich humus floor.

Curious eyes watch the shadow's passing—watch dry leaves eddy and whisper in the long cloak's wake. Small ears twitch, listening to soft melodies drifting and dancing in the beams of sunlight shafting down through the trees.

A young woman is kneading bread dough in one of the houses. A wisp of hair escapes from her headscarf, and there is flour on her cheeks.

She pauses, balefully eyeing the dough. Her bread-making never seems to go right, and her husband scolds her incessantly for it.

Thinking about her husband produces a crooked smile.

Her husband isn't a cruel man, but he is stern, with no tolerance for foolishness. He also has a temper that she tries very hard not to provoke. *Without too much success, unfortunately.*

They were partnered as husband and wife by the Code Keeper, as is the custom. It could have been worse. He could have partnered her with the Animal Keeper, who reeks of the livestock in his care. She and the other women can tell when the Animal Keeper is approaching if a breeze is blowing and they are downwind. A snort of laughter escapes her. However, she quickly suppresses it. Frivolity is a sin. *Like just about everything else.* She punches down into the dough.

Her thoughts turn to her son.

He is attending education in the schoolhouse with the other lads, and proving to be a son his father is proud of— quick to learn and quietly obedient. He will do well when he takes on his father's role in the future.

All boys follow the occupation of their fathers, whatever that trade happens to be:—carpenter, weaver, blacksmith, tailor, grower, and such.

The Founder gave every man a role when they were getting the settlement established. The men's roles were designed to cover the practical needs of the community for all time. There are no deviations from the system.

It doesn't matter if a young boy has dreams of doing something else. Boys learn very quickly that having dreams is futile. Whatever family he is born into, that is what he will be.

Her thoughts drift back to her son.

He's their first child, and she loves him dearly. However, as a mother, she finds it difficult not being able to show her affection openly. Displays of affection are forbidden, being considered an *emotional weakness*, by those in authority.

"Piffle and nonsense!" she snaps crossly and gives the dough a hearty thump.

The young wife ponders her upbringing and the role women have in their community.

Females do not receive a formal education, for it is considered a waste of time. The purpose of a woman, according to their leaders, is to "keep house, produce offspring, and obey her husband."

The young woman's expression darkens, and the bread dough comes under vigorous attack. She puts out her hand, to steady a pitcher of water which is threatening to fall off the quivering table.

Staring down at the beleaguered lump of dough, she sighs. *No wonder it never turns out right.* Her (almost) indigestible bread must be reflecting her anger and frustrations. *It's an interesting thought.*

The sound of somebody pounding on the street door breaks in on her musings, and she runs to see who it is. When she opens the door, her face turns as white as the flour on her hands. *Stalwarts!*

The two servants of the Great House stare at her for a moment, before shouldering her aside.

Chapter 4

"Sin must be cast out."

The tall, cloaked figure steps out from the forest trees. Blue-green eyes study the surrounding scene from the shadows of the cloak's cowl hood.

A massive escarpment curves around the great plateau, giving it the appearance of a vast amphitheater. Evergreen trees of all shades and kinds, climb in close ranks toward the peaks. Others march resolutely downward from the edge of the plateau to the hills and lands below.

A solitary eagle glides high overhead, its shrill cries echoing across the blue expanse.

Movement catches the figure's attention.

A gray rabbit is sitting up, its nose twitching, and its senses on full alert. Soft, brown eyes regard the visitor for a moment, and then the rabbit resumes its foraging. It knows it is in no danger. Not from him.

Some distance away, at the foot of the escarpment, a faint pall of blue-grey smoke can be seen. In front of him there is a trail leading off into the meadow grass and gently waving crops.

The cloaked stranger hums softly to himself, as he sets off on the path.

"Not long now," he murmurs.

The Meeting room of the Great House is not a place where Joy or Gladness can while away a pleasant hour.

Despair and Resignation, on the other hand, are always right at home.

The Code Keeper sweeps in, throwing a cursory glance at the Elders who are sitting along the narrow wall-bench. All they know is that someone has committed a grave sin, and the Keeper requires their presence, as protocol dictates.

The Code Keeper smiles coldly to himself, hearing the nervous clearing of throats and anxious shuffling of feet as he strides past the waiting men.

At one end of the large Meeting room, there is a podium on which a wooden lectern stands. Resting on the stand is a large book. It is the Book of Judgments and the fourth of its kind. The Code Keeper mounts the podium and opens the massive tome. These are books which command respect, for written within are the disciplines and judgments made by Code Keepers, going right back to the days of the Founder. The books are wonderful sources of reference when it comes to dealing with breaches of the Code, and other issues. *His* entries are, of course, included.

The Meeting room door creaks open, and the Stalwarts enter.

When the Elders see who they are escorting, several can't help a sharp intake of breath. What on earth, did the Teachers wife do to land herself here, of all places? They'd have thought that avoiding the Great House would have been the highest priority in her life, past things considered.

The Healer has taken up his position near the Code Keeper and is standing with his hands clasped behind his back, contemplating the young woman. He mentally runs through a list of eligible females, in case there is a need to replace her.

The Stalwarts position the Teacher's wife before the podium and hand the confiscated package to the Code

Keeper. He removes the contents of the package carefully. Being Code Keeper, he is above being corrupted and can handle sinful objects with impunity.

"Look up!"

The Keeper's angry shout startles her. She looks at the fragile items he is holding out in the palm of his hand.

"*These* were found secreted in your house. You are the one who hid them are you not?"

The Teacher's wife nods. There is no point denying it.

The Keeper leans forward, and his voice is chilling.

"You *know* what happens to those who break the Code!"

The silence in the room is almost palpable. The Teacher's wife is trembling, her fear of the Code Keeper well founded.

"Not saying anything? I'd have thought you'd have some interesting excuse as to why you have so blatantly sinned!"

She hears the sly challenge. However, she's heard such challenges in the past and suffered the consequences of responding; she remains silent. Her thoughts turn to her *crime.*

Every morning, the Pickers patrol the village, tearing up plants that bear the bright colors of sin.

However, a few days ago they overlooked a pocket of flowers growing behind her home. Nobody else was around, so she'd picked the flowers and hidden them in her apron.

Going back inside, she had carefully placed the flowers between two pieces of parchment, then wrapped them up in a scrap of hessian. She'd hidden the package under the vegetable box, thinking it would be safe.

When her husband and son were absent, she would bring the flowers out, so she could admire their petals and bright colors. They'd been a secret source of delight. She'd thought, foolishly, that she could keep them hidden forever.

A flash of defiance momentarily overrides her fear. *I refuse to believe that colors are sinful, and how can picking flowers be a crime? That's so stupid!* The Teacher's wife bites her lip. Some of the women believe that Code Keepers can read thoughts. *She* doesn't believe it, but...?

The Code Keeper's voice thunders out, making her jump.

"You have committed a major sin—the sin of *rebellion*. The Code says, "Rebellion is as the sin of witchcraft." You know this!"

The Teacher's wife turns icy cold at his words. The seriousness of her situation is now dawning upon her.

The Keeper has been watching the play of emotions. He can't read thoughts, but he can read faces. *Oh yes, he can read faces very well. Hers in particular.*

"You know that Fiery Judgment fell upon the world below because of such sins. Do you want to bring a similar judgment down upon us?"

The Teacher's wife shakes her head.

The Code Keeper sighs angrily.

"You have always questioned and had difficulty submitting."

The Keeper leans on the lectern, hands clasped together as if in prayer.

"I thought you would settle down once you were partnered with the Teacher and had a child. However, it appears I was wrong."

Her heart pounds. Something terrible is coming. She *knows* it.

The Keeper straightens up and hands the package to the Healer, who will include it in the next day's Burning. He turns back to the young woman and gazes down at her, his eyes hard and his face grim.

"You have a wayward spirit. By this last rebellious act, you have forfeited your right to be a member of this holy community."

A gasp escapes her. *He wouldn't, would he?* She risks a glance upward. His expression is dark, thunderous. *Yes, he would!*

In a cold, angry voice, he confirms her worst fear.

"You will be driven out at first light tomorrow, with no provisions of any kind. You will have the clothes that are upon you now, and that is all. There will be no farewells. Nobody will be permitted to watch you leave. Your fate will be in the hands of Divine Providence!"

The Teacher's wife sways, and she puts out a hand for support. However, no support is there.

The Code Keeper enters the sin and judgment in the book, then places both hands on either side of the lectern. In a stern voice, he addresses the men in the room.

"Sin must be cast out! Amen?"

"Amen," is the collective response. (They wouldn't dare say anything else.)

Without a further glance at the Teacher's wife the Keeper steps down from the podium and strides toward the door. Just as he is about to pass through, an anguished cry rings out.

"Father!"

The cry hits the Keeper between the shoulder blades like a hammer blow. For a split second, he hesitates, however, it is a split second only. He shrugs his shoulders as if to dispel an annoying itch, steps through the doorway, and is gone.

The Healer follows close behind, his mind already working on the contingency plan.

The Teacher's wife stands very still as if turned to stone. She struggles to hold back the surging emotions.

The Elders file out of the room. None of them dare look at her. They are too ashamed. The Code Keeper has made a cruel call, and they are powerless to do anything about it. Sickened by their cowardice, the Elders leave the building, appalled that the community is going to lose another member.

As soon as the Elders have left, the Stalwarts take the Teacher's wife to a small cell at the rear of the building. They manacle her to a length of chain that is attached to an iron ring on the wall. Without a word, the Stalwarts exit the cell, closing the door behind them with a loud '*thud.*'

The Teacher's wife looks at her surroundings in despair. She had hoped never to see this room again.

A tiny barred window set high on the back wall gives the only opportunity for light. There is no furnishing in the room apart from a bucket nearby. It is a room designed for short-term tenancy.

During her growing years, she spent many hours, and occasionally, days and nights, within its stark walls. Always for some *perceived* sin, or a failure to measure up.

She sits on the floor, her back against the wall. The face of her young son fills her mind and pain floods through her. The realization that she will never see him again turns the pain into a howling beast that rips and tears with sharp claws.

The black bird of Anger suddenly surges up on furiously beating wings. *Why don't the men confront the leaders, and do something about the brutal system?*

Even as Anger rages, the Teacher's wife knows the answer. It is fear! Deep, abiding fear. Fear that has been bred into them from a tender age and reinforced on a daily basis.

The black bird of Anger beats its wings in frantic desperation until, thoroughly exhausted, it falls into a pool of despair and drowns.

Chapter 5

A Timeless Face

He is standing on the boundary where the meadow grass ends, and the dust of the village proper begins. Stretching before him is a broad street with simple buildings forming a guard of honor along both sides. He can make out other buildings behind and beyond.

All the dwellings are identical—gray weathered timber and gray shingle rooftops. From chimneys of gray stone, blue-gray wisps of smoke make feeble attempts at escape. Beside each door, there is a single window, through which the houses gaze at each other in mute silence.

Further along the dusty street, there is a large round water trough, with walls of dark hewn stone. An iron pump stands on the far side like a silent sentinel; water drops glistening on its pouting lower lip.

Beyond the water trough is a building considerably larger than the others. It is a building commanding a view of the whole street.

The stranger's face is grim. The scene before him has all the warmth of a smile painted on a bear-trap. Still...

He enters the village, his cloak flowing in soft folds about him. All is eerily quiet, except for faint sounds of industry from the buildings beyond the houses. No children are playing outside, and no neighbors are sharing life events on doorsteps.

Arriving at the water trough, the stranger settles himself on the stone wall and closes his eyes. He is *listening* to the village.

After some moments the stranger pushes back the hood of his cloak and in a voice that is soft, with mellow flutes in its undertones, he begins to sing.

In shades of yellow, lilac, and pink, the lovely song dances through the oppressive atmosphere of the village, the bright notes shimmering, like gems in the sunlight.

Busy hands pause in their activities. Heads turn and whispered conversations cease. After a moment, however, shoulders shrug and activities are resumed. *It's just the wind singing through the eaves.*

In the large building at the head of the street, there is a different reaction.

The Code Keeper is sitting at his desk meditating, the window open to let in some fresh air. As the lovely notes drift into his office, he leaps to his feet so violently that his chair topples over. The gentle melody is tugging at his soul in the same way that snagging thorns and briers pull at clothing.

The Code Keeper snatches up his silver-handled horsewhip *Righteousness*, and heads for the front door, shouting more to himself, than to anybody else: "*This* is why music is forbidden. It is an *evil* that stirs up trouble and corrupts the soul!"

He steps outside the building and immediately spots the stranger sitting on the wall of the water trough. The angry Keeper strides up to the man.

"Stop that infernal sound this instant!"

The Keeper stands over him, *Righteousness* at the ready.

The stranger falls silent. He gazes up at the Keeper, seeing the darkness coiled inside.

The Code Keeper stares at the intruder, seeing a vagrant, a trespasser; *an evil influence!* His hand tightens on *Righteousness*, knuckles turning white.

"Who are you? Why are you here?"

The stranger idly stirs the water in the trough with his fingers, as if he hasn't heard the Code Keeper.

The Code Keeper's eyes widen in disbelief. Nobody, but nobody, ignores *him*!

The furious Keeper stares at the stranger, noting the wavy brown hair and face tanned brown by the sun. There is nothing remarkable about the man, except for his eyes. They are a striking blue-green color. The Keeper has never seen eyes of that color before.

The man's age is hard to determine. He has a youthfulness about him, yet the Keeper is getting a sense of *age* as well. The word *timeless* drops into the Keeper's mind. However, he swats the word away as he would an irritating fly.

A second time, the Code Keeper asks the stranger for his name and again, receives no response.

The Keeper is now close to losing his temper.

"Pay attention to me! I am the Head of this community and the highest Authority. I insist you answer me immediately!"

The stranger turns his head away to hide an amused smile.

The Code Keeper is fed up. The intruder doesn't have a clue who he's dealing with, and it's time he let the man know!

The Keeper opens his mouth to convey what he's thinking, but as he does, those disturbing blue-green eyes glance up. The Keeper's mouth snaps shut with an audible '*clack*.'

For the first time in his life, the Keeper finds himself at a complete loss for words, and it puts him in a foul mood. He storms back into the Great House, bellowing for the Healer and Stalwarts to join him in his office. They run to obey.

Back at the water trough, the stranger calmly resumes his singing.

Menfolk and students are now making their way home. The Teacher and his son are among them.

They see the stranger, and their steps falter. Strangers don't stumble into their community that often, however, when they do, ugly situations always follow.

The concerned men are further distressed by the stranger's singing, for it is stirring up emotions; emotions that disturb and frighten them.

The men quicken their pace, dragging students along with them. They don't want the boys too distracted by the stranger's presence. Nobody will communicate with the stranger, for to do so, would bring Stalwarts knocking on their doors. The nervous men and disappointed students disappear inside their homes.

The stranger decides to take a quiet walk along the length of the street, while it's empty. As he walks, he listens; listens to the music playing in the souls of the people.

There is the gray discordant song of fear singing hand in hand with catawba[2] songs of sadness. He hears sable songs of oppression, singing in harmony with graphite cruelty. Sorrow, despair, and hopelessness add their voices, singing jangling refrains of obsidian, ebony, and sickly yellow.

The stranger groans.

"These are not the songs *I* sang to them. These are songs which others have forced upon them."

It would be so easy for him to surge into their lives and cut loose against the foul music of darkness. However, he will not do it. Bruised reeds do not need a heavy boot adding yet more pain to their already damaged lives.

Patience, compassion and above all—love.

"That is *my* song...among others," he cries softly. "As for those who wear heavy boots..."

The stranger now strides purposefully toward the Great House.

Chapter 6

"We are the people of the Code."

The Stalwart hastily responds to the knocking on the door. Seeing who is standing outside, he promptly runs to inform the Code Keeper.

Annoyed at the stranger's audacity, the Keeper rages out of the Meeting room, determined to drag the man into the other cell. His plans are put on hold, however, when he sees the man pointing at something nearby.

His interest piqued, the Code Keeper turns to look and sees that the plaque on the wall is what's drawing the stranger's attention. Carved into the thick wooden plaque, are the words:

'THE CODE GIVETH LIFE.'

The Keeper smiles coldly to himself as the germ of an idea takes shape. If the stranger wants to know more about those sacred words, then why not oblige him? It might be refreshing to tell somebody else about their holy heritage. *It's not as if the stranger will be taking the information anywhere.*

The Stalwart is waiting to see what the Code Keeper intends to do. He can't help a grim smile as he wonders what the stranger would do if he knew that those who stumble into their village, never have the option of stumbling back out again. Code Keepers are worse than rabid wolves when it comes to protecting what belongs to them.

The Stalwart can't believe it when he hears the Code Keeper *inviting* the stranger into the Great House. It's not the invitation that shocks him so much; it's how the Code Keeper is presenting it. He's using a friendly, polite tone of voice that the Stalwart has *never* heard before. The Keeper is even using friendly gestures! *What's he doing?*

The Keeper and his *guest* enter the building. The Stalwart recovers and follows the two men inside.

The Healer and the other Stalwart stare in amazement as the trio enter the Keeper's office.

The Keeper *asks* all of the men to leave but also requests that they not go far because he will require their services later. They understand what he is communicating to them. The three men head off to another room, muttering about the Keeper's strange *friendly* behavior.

Once they have gone, the Code Keeper sits down at his desk and invites the stranger to have a seat. Putting his hand on the old book, which is still lying on the desktop, the Keeper begins relating the history of the village, in tones befitting a *Trauermarsch*[3].

"We are the people of the Code."

He taps the book with his fingertips.

"This book is where life begins and ends for our sacred community. It is a holy Copy of our Founder's *original* book. A book called, *the Code.* Divine Agents wrote this Copy themselves, before taking the Founder's holy book into Heaven for safe keeping."

The Keeper looks over at the stranger. The man is sitting with his head bowed, elbows on the chair's armrests, and his fingers steepled. He appears to be listening carefully.

The Code Keeper continues his narration, the level of his voice rising to meet that of his pride.

"This sacred Copy of the Code has been passed from Keeper to Keeper, over many generations. Only we Code Keepers have the right to read, and teach from its sacred pages."

The Keeper pauses. He could swear that he heard soft humming a moment ago. The Keeper listens intently, however, he hears nothing and concludes that he must have been imagining it.

In an even louder voice, the Keeper continues.

"Our holy community was founded by *my* ancestor. He was the first Code Keeper; a devout and holy man who..."

The Keeper is interrupted by a cough, and he asks his guest if he is alright? Not out of concern, but because he was interrupted.

The stranger, with an odd smile on his face, waves his hand for the Keeper to continue.

(He's not going to let on that the Keeper's description of his "devout and holy" ancestor has stuck in his craw.)

"My saintly ancestor, (another cough from the stranger) vexed by the wickedness of those around him, came under the firm conviction that...that..."

The Keeper's voice fades as his mind begins drifting, in the manner of a leaf drifting on a stream.

While the stranger quietly watches, the Keeper's head drops back, his mouth sags open, and very soon the sound of snoring is heard.

The stranger grins. *Snooze away, dear friend, snooze away. I already know the history of your community, and I'm not talking about the fictional version.*

He settles himself more comfortably in the chair and hums softly, while the real history of the community passes before him like a living diorama, every ugly detail in full view.

CHAPTER 7

The Founder

The Founder's name was *Abraham Silas Pope*. A man with as much tenderness and warmth as tempered steel.

He had been raised in an environment more like that of an *iron foundry* than a 'home.'

Pope's paternal grandparents and his father were the three dominating characters who controlled this *foundry*. All three possessed hearts like blast furnaces; hearts that had burned white-hot with the belief that young Pope endure "smelting and refining processes," to be an heir worthy of the Pope name. Their dedicated efforts produced results beyond even *their* expectations!

Like a dull-winged moth emerging from its equally dull chrysalis, Pope emerged from youth into adulthood: excessively pious, uncompromising, unforgiving and merciless. As if those *qualities* weren't enough, Pope was also ruthless, and highly intolerant of all who moved outside the sphere of *himself*.

As the years passed, it became apparent to Pope that his hope of being independent, and free of the tyrannical rule of his seniors, was slipping away. Pope kept his resentment and anger hidden, however, for he had the belief that Divine Providence would one day provide a way out.

Not long after Pope's thirty-seventh birthday, a horrific event occurred.

It was the family's custom to conduct personal business meetings in an upstairs room of a local establishment situated on the outer edge of town.

One night, during one of these sessions, a fire broke out in a downstairs storeroom. The fire spread so rapidly that those upstairs didn't stand a chance. They perished in the raging inferno.

Pope himself, managed to escape. He was not present when the fire broke out, having left the meeting early for some reason or another.

The tragedy shocked the townsfolk. Key pillars of their community had been wiped out in one fell swoop. They watched to see what Pope would do, now that he was the sole surviving family member.

When the tedious round of tributes, hymns, and prayers was finally over, Pope ensconced himself in the family solicitors' office. Against all advice, he systematically offloaded businesses, investments, and properties, for prices and values that would have had the Pope seniors rising from their ashy graves in a furious rage.

Hungry buyers flocked like greedy vultures, keen to get their share of the lucrative pickings. Many of them squabbled and came to blows as they fought over the meatier portions.

The only property retained by Pope was the family home, for which he had specific plans.

After contracts were signed, sealed and final payments delivered, Pope emptied all bank accounts.

What he did with the funds, became the subject of wild speculation and gossip. Pope didn't care. He found a perverse pleasure in the fact that he had the whole town in a state of confusion and bewilderment.

Pope was now free! Free to act on convictions that had been blazing in him for some time.

First, was the unshakeable belief that humanity was thundering toward damnation in the same way that stampeding cattle rush headlong toward the edge of a cliff. The citizens of his town, in particular.

Following that, was the conviction that Divine Providence had had enough! Fiery Judgment was on its way. The clouds were going to rend apart, and Divine Wrath was going to fall!

Pope's biggest conviction of all, however, was that the *anointing* of ancient prophets was upon him. He was Jonah, Isaiah, and Jeremiah; all rolled into one.

Pope believed he had been singularly *chosen* to warn the people that: if they wanted to escape Divine retribution, they would need to repent and follow *him* to true righteousness. *He* would be the author of their salvation.

Filled with a holy *determination* against sin and sinners, he took to the streets, roads, and alleyways of the town. Any place where people congregated. He even targeted the town's long-established church that, according to Pope, showed more interest in preserving the resting places of the dead than it did in maintaining the souls of the living!

Pope was well armed for his campaign against sin and unrighteousness. As he preached, he wielded a silver-handled horsewhip named *Righteousness* in one hand, and a black leather-covered book he called *the Code,* in the other.

Righteousness had formerly been the pride and joy of Pope's grandfather. The old man had passed the horsewhip on to his son Silas (Pope's father), who had consequently passed it on to Abraham at his coming of age.

The much-cherished horsewhip had been used effectively to *save* Pope when he was young, so Pope knew without a shadow of a doubt, that *Righteousness* would be *useful* in 'saving' others.

With his black broad-brimmed hat crammed on his head and his long black coat flapping behind him, Pope stalked through the town, looking for all the world, like a giant crow; his enthusiastic preaching no doubt sounding like wild *cawing.*

At first, many of the people regarded Pope and his fiery preaching as a joke, something to laugh about over their ale. Many would whoop with laughter on the occasions Pope chased them, waving the horsewhip, and shouting vehement warnings about their "festering" souls. It wasn't long, however, before the people began to view Pope as an irritation, an annoying presence on their streets.

Those who had received cracks across the shoulders from *Righteousness,* along with insults and verbal abuse, demanded Pope be put away as a public nuisance. They could put up with it happening once or twice, but after numerous run-ins, they'd had enough.

Matrons and mothers, heartily sick of having their young charges reduced to tears, developed a strategy of their own. As soon as Pope began terrifying the young ones with descriptions of hellfire and torment, the women would attack him furiously with bags, brollies or walking canes. They were having none of his nonsense, thank you very much!

Some of them even turned their precious "poochikins" onto Pope. Said *poochikins* had no hesitation in latching onto Pope's trousers or dangling coat-tails, and it took some effort on Pope's part, to dislodge the "mongrels." Once dislodged, Pope would follow through with a vicious kick aimed at any part of the mutt's anatomy that his boot could reach.

During his forays through the town, Pope also discovered that young women did not take kindly to being told they looked like "hussies" in their fashionable clothing. When Pope launched into verbal assaults on their fashion sense, these young women expressed their outrage so vociferously, that the ancient gods of war, would have been pounding on their shields while roaring approval from the sidelines.

Encouraged by the actions of the adults, young boys would bombard Pope with small stones or rotten fruit. Sometimes they would run up and kick him in the shins, before darting away, to hide behind any available cover.

Pope got used to returning home with his clothes dirty and splattered, and his dignity in much the same state.

Despite the derision he suffered, Pope carried on undaunted. As far as he was concerned, the more the opposition, the greater the Heavenly rewards. Hallelujah!

How the people put up with Pope for as long as they did, is anybody's guess. Perhaps it was because his grandfather had been a Founding Father. It may have been because the Pope family had, over time, brought lucrative business to the town. Whatever the reasons, nobody did him any serious harm. Most just chose to stay out of his way if they could. In other words, the town tolerated him.

Pope pushed that tolerance to its limit, however, by gate-crashing a meeting of the Town Elders one sultry evening.

Charging in, he began snatching up official documents, tossing them left, right, and center. While he was doing that, he loudly denounced the illustrious Town Elders, branding them as "followers of the devil," who were more interested in lining their pockets, than working for the good of the people.

(The fact that he may have been right was beside the point. It was the attacks on their dignity and pride that were unforgivable.)

Livid with rage, the Town Elders physically dragged Pope out of the building and hurled him into the street, ordering men nearby to toss "the lunatic" into the nearest horse trough. An order which was promptly carried out with undisguised relish.

Pope hauled himself out of the trough, dripping wet, and shaking with cold.

As he squelched back to the family residence, Pope loudly informed whoever could hear, that he was done with the lot of them and wouldn't care if they all went up in smoke.

Wanting to see what the shouting was about, folk opened their windows. They couldn't help grinning when they heard what Pope was saying.

"Goodbye and good riddance yourself!" they shouted out of their windows, before returning to their warm beds.

When Pope arrived at the grand old family home, he quickly set about harnessing a team of horses to one of the wagons, which he then filled with various items. Once satisfied he had everything he needed he went back inside. There was a final task to complete.

Beginning on the upper floor, Pope passed through every room, emptying paraffin oil lamps, tossing their flammable contents over walls and furnishings. He threw in lit tapers, and it wasn't long before the house was ablaze from top to bottom.

Pope couldn't help indulging himself—he did something he'd never done before. He *laughed.* The sight of his miserable childhood existence going up in flames was glorious! He was thrilled to finally be giving the "rotten pile" the attention it so richly deserved.

After that, confident in the knowledge that he had done all that the Divine required of him, he shook the dust off his shoes to show he was done with the place, whipped up his horses, and disappeared into the night.

When he was a couple of kilometers from the town, Pope pulled his horses to a halt and turned for a last look.

Pope stared, mesmerized by the lurid glow of flames filling the sky; a glow that was spreading rapidly. The fire had evidently taken hold and like a ravenous beast was leaping from building to building. Faint cries and screams carried to him on the night breeze.

As Pope gazed at the devastation *he* had set in motion, fear attempted to gain entrance. Pope stamped on the foolish emotion immediately. He had merely been an *instrument* in the hands of the Divine.

CHAPTER 8

Protocol and Herbal Tea

In the Great House, the Code Keeper jerks awake and is horrified. He'd dozed off! *Unthinkable!*

Out of sorts, the Keeper rummages around the desktop for his flint so he can light the candles. When the room is aglow with their flickering light, the Keeper looks to see if his guest is still present. The stranger is there, apparently unconcerned that his host has been dozing.

The stranger nods and smiles at the Keeper, who shifts uncomfortably. Smiles are suspect. *Who knows what is hidden behind a smile.*

Mildly flustered, the Keeper shuffles parchments. As he does, he informs his visitor that he'll have the Healer bring in a beaker of herbal tea.

The stranger nods and gives the Keeper another one of his unsettling smiles. (He knows what they have planned for him. Not that their plans will do them a scrap of good.)

The Code Keeper leaves the room to give orders to the other men, who have been waiting elsewhere. When the Keeper returns, he retakes his seat behind the desk.

Silence fills the room as both men quietly contemplate each other. The Keeper muses that it must be the quietest confrontation with a stranger in the history of the community.

The Healer duly arrives, places the ordered brew on the Keeper's desk, then steps back and waits.

Quiet moments pass.

The Keeper is still pondering the stranger. In particular, the man's complete lack of verbal communication. All they've heard is his singing. *That's* not a form of communication at all. Maybe the man doesn't like talking much. He might be one of those people who has spent so much time on their own, that they find themselves *unable* to communicate with others. Whatever the reason, he's not going to get anything out of the stranger, that's very clear.

The Healer is tired of waiting around and clears his throat noisily.

The sound snaps the Keeper back to attention. He looks over at the stranger and finds those blue-green eyes watching him carefully. An ice-cold finger traces a delicate path down the Keeper's spine, and he shivers; *what is it about this man?*

The Keeper hears the Healer's voice booming in his ear, reminding him of the tea. He stares at the brew for a few seconds before impatiently pushing it aside. *Enough! By the Code, my head is pounding, and I just want some peace!* The Code Keeper makes a bold decision which he knows is going to ruffle the Healer's feathers.

Calling for the Stalwarts, he orders them to escort the stranger to the forest, and let him go.

As predicted, the Healer's face registers shock, and his eyebrows shoot upward.

The Keeper is so out of sorts that he doesn't care.

The stranger rises to his feet and extends his hand to the Keeper, as politeness would usually dictate.

The Keeper looks at the tendered hand. Gritting his teeth, he touches the stranger's fingers, intending to have as little contact as possible. However, to his horror, his hand is clasped firmly. A shock passes through the Keeper, and he snatches his hand away, unconsciously wiping it on his coat, as if to remove something distasteful.

The stranger's mouth twitches upward, and his eyes dance. However, the flustered Code Keeper doesn't notice.

After the Stalwarts and the stranger have left, the Keeper leans back in his chair. He glances across at the Healer.

"You have a problem?"

The Healer gestures toward the brew.

"Take it away; we don't need it!" the Keeper snaps.

The Healer returns to his quarters, taking the unwanted concoction with him. He cannot understand the Keeper's decision. Their Protocols state very clearly that after the potent brew has taken effect, the unlucky victim, is to be taken into the forest and left, so wild animals can finish the job. It is an efficient system that has worked since the founding of their community. The drastic measures are necessary, to ensure their holy community remains free of corruption.

While the Healer puzzles over the out of character decision of the Keeper, the Stalwarts accompany the stranger through the fields, their flaming torches casting eerie shadows around them.

When they reach the boundary of the forest, the Stalwarts warn him to leave the plateau and never return. They watch him disappear into the woods.

Satisfied, they return to the village, hoping that hungry wolves or bears will take care of the matter for them.

CHAPTER 9

Specter in the Night

Moonlight paints the village and surrounding scenery in silver. The cry of a night bird echoes across the plateau. The sharp barking of a fox drifts faintly on the evening breeze. From the Animal yards, come soft whinnies, gentle lowing, and the shifting of penned animals.

The Code Keeper is standing out on the trail behind the Great House, hoping that the cold air will reduce the pounding in his head. He gazes at the nearby crops, dancing with moonlight and shadows, his thoughts dwelling on the Founder and other things.

The Founder's devotion to the Code has always been an inspiration. Not just to himself, but to all Code Keepers. His father had been formidable in his adherence to the rules set in stone by the Founder.

The Keeper thinks of his son, who is now a young man. He has reached the end of his schoolhouse education and will shortly begin serving in an *apprentice* capacity, actively learning how to lead and govern the community. He's been preparing the lad for years. However, it will take the experience to cement him into his future role. Perhaps he is a fraction too hard in his disciplining at times. However, that is the way things are. His son knows it and accepts it.

A deep frown creases the Code Keeper's face.

He hopes the boy will not display any of his mother's weaknesses in the future. That would be disastrous. The woman had been a veritable thorn in his side. Her untimely death, though sad and inconvenient, had given him the freedom to raise his two offspring without her silly concerns and constant questioning acting as constraints.

The Keeper draws his thick coat closer. A cold wind has risen. There are rustlings in the fields, and the wind is moaning through the tops of nearby trees.

A small sound catches his attention. *Did he just hear singing?* The Keeper listens intently. He walks further along the path, straining to hear. *Yes, there it is again.* He can hear the faint sound of singing coming from somewhere up ahead.

A gust of wind races through the crops nearby, causing them to rattle and swish, as if a giant hand is brushing across them—back and forth, back and forth.

"Keeper..."

It sounds like a sigh on the wind.

The Keeper's scalp prickles. He stares out into the darkness but can see nothing. Fear prods him with its bony finger. He tries to shake it off by telling himself he imagined the voice.

"Keeper..."

The deep, musical voice speaks directly into his ear.

The Keeper leaps like a startled deer and sets off, running back to the village, at a fast gallop. He hunches forward as he runs, imagining that at any moment, he is going to feel the cold grip of some terrifying *specter* on the back of his neck.

The frightened Code Keeper reaches the rear door of the Great House, yanks it open, and falls inside. Pulling the door shut, he quickly slams the bolt home. When his heart stops yammering, he walks on unsteady legs to his office, and sits down in the one place he feels truly safe—behind the large desk. *By the Code, what was that?* The Keeper picks up a quill for something to do. However, his hands are shaking so badly that he drops it.

The Founder was right! Singing is a lure. Look at how the singing enticed him away from the safety of the village. If he had not run, who knows what might have happened.

The frazzled Keeper picks up the Code. Reading should calm his jangling nerves.

The Keeper wonders how the Founder dealt with apparitions and specters. How did *he* respond when frightening events occurred? How did he feel when he saw his town going up in flames in Fiery Judgment? That alone must have been terrifying. *How did the Founder cope with such things?*

Chapter 10

The Founder's Flock

As Pope watched his predictions of Fiery Judgment coming true, he was close to a state of euphoria. *Who would doubt him now?*

Pope wondered if there would be any survivors, apart from himself. The thought crossed his mind that it was entirely possible, and he mulled over what plans the Divine might have for *them*.

As he deliberated, the answer came in a flash of revelation: those who escaped the flames would be a *holy remnant*, chosen by the Divine to be a new and holy people. Just like those who survived the Great Flood.

As Pope thought on these things, he had a Vision. A Vision in which he saw himself forging these saved souls into godly men and women, through his teachings from the Code and the sanctifying applications of *Righteousness*.

Filled with excitement, Pope couldn't help giving an exultant shout before taking off along the moonlit trail once more. There was no need for him to wait. Divine Providence would bring them to him.

It happened that two hundred and sixty-five souls made their escape from the burning town. While others fled to the coast or took paths to the south, these folk fled to the surrounding farmlands, hauling everything they'd been able to grab; on foot, in hastily loaded wagons, and on horseback.

In varying states of dress and distress, they stood in the fields, watching the merciless flames devouring town and homes. Wives were weeping as they tried to console frightened, wide-eyed children. Older folk held each other, wondering how they would survive. Men quietly surveyed the nightmare scene and began considering their options. Young people, though shocked and frightened, couldn't help feeling that it was all a bit of an adventure. Such was their nature.

Eventually, animated discussions began to fly back and forth regarding their future. Pope's predictions had come true, so one and all agreed that it might be prudent to seek him out. He might have some answers for them. It was not as if they had anything to lose by going after him. Decision made, they formed a rag-tag procession and took to the trail, believing that Pope couldn't be that far off.

They didn't know Pope. He had set a furious pace, stopping only to give his horses an occasional rest. He had a Divine purpose, and he wasn't going to let anything or anyone slow him down.

It took a few days, but finally, the exhausted, bedraggled survivors found him camped in a broad expanse of lush green grass dotted with wildflowers. A stream meandered through the scene. Their noisy arrival caused a stirring up of wildfowl and rabbits.

The tired people gathered around Pope, thanking him for his warnings—warnings which they admitted they should have heeded. They then asked Pope if he had any counsel or guidance to give them.

Pope had watched the people drifting in and had sent up a word of thanks to Divine Providence. They might look a miserable lot, however, if *these* were the ones chosen to be his Flock, then by the Code, he would do whatever it took, to make them shining beacons of righteousness.

He announced that the Divine had already spoken to him about their future. He also informed them that the Divine had chosen *them* for salvation and that a place of blessing and prosperity awaited them *if* they would place themselves under *his* authority, and leadership.

The people liked the idea of being *chosen* for good things. There was a ring of *destiny* to it. The devastation of their town had been extreme, so maybe the *blessings* would be of an extraordinary nature, being the opposite end of the scale?

After a brief debate, the people decided to accept Pope's offer of a new life under his leadership, and yes, (sigh), they would listen to his preaching and teaching.

For two days, Pope let the people rest in the peaceful surroundings. They needed to become more familiar with the practical aspects of life on the trail.

On the morning of the third day, their leader rose up while it was still dark, the glow of dawn a mere promise. Walking around the campsites, he shouted for them to get up and make ready for departure.

After hasty preparations, the people were finally lined up.

Pope climbed onto his wagon, where he stood surveying the hopefuls. Spreading his arms wide, he made a passionate proclamation.

"We now begin our real journey. We will not stop until we come to the place chosen for us. It will be shown to me and me alone, for I am the one with the Vision. As for you, you are now the people of the Code, the *Chosen*. The journey will be long, and there will no doubt be hardship. However, endure to the end, and you will reap great blessings and rewards."

The people were not too sure about the "hardship" aspect. However, they did enjoy hearing about those "blessings and rewards."

Before they headed out up the trail, Pope selected three men to assist him in the enormous task ahead.

One, he appointed to be the *Healer,* for Pope had discovered that this particular individual had an extensive knowledge of herbs, and experience in medicinal applications. The Healer would be his second in command.

Two other men were appointed to serve both himself and the Healer. *Their* qualifications were that they both had the build and personalities of bullocks. They would be known as *Stalwarts.*

The people were now feeling very positive. Things were happening. Everything was going to be alright.

Keen to get to their destination, which they hoped wouldn't be *that* far away, the Chosen faced forward, with smiles on their faces, and excitement in their hearts.

Chapter 11

Moonlight and Shadows

At the edge of the plateau, in the dark shadows of the forest trees, there is a shift, a change. A tall figure steps out, his cloak of moonlight and shadows, flowing about him.

Moving silently, he follows the border between plateau and forest until he arrives at the fast flowing mountain stream. In one lithe movement, he leaps up onto a large boulder, where he sits listening to the sounds around him.

The stream's swiftly flowing water sings joyfully, as it bubbles and foams around the bounder's base. A wolf howls its sad refrain, somewhere in the depths of the forest. The cool mountain breeze sighs, ruffling the surface of the water with its breath. Rustlings can be heard as small creatures go about their nocturnal activities, alert to any larger animals or winged attackers from above.

A warm smile fills the stranger's face. These are the songs of life. Every creature, small or great, has its unique voice and melody; one that adds to the theme and luster of Creation's orchestra.

He gazes up at the star-filled skies and laughs.

"Yes, you are all exquisite...and you are also very loud!"

He turns his head sharply, detecting another sound. One he knows all too well. It is the insidious music of the *Other*.

"*You're* in for a surprise," he murmurs. "You're not going to like it, but then, you never do."

Rising to his feet, he faces toward the sleeping settlement and begins to sing.

His melody, though simple in structure, is rich with color; a veritable palette of vibrant notes and phrases.

The message in his song is direct and full of purpose.

The *Other* stirs restlessly, feeling a faint foreign harmony. It hums back along its threads, seeking what is causing the vibration, the agitation among its notes. However, believing fully in its inviolability, the *Other* only makes a half-hearted effort. "It's nothing," the *Other* mumbles, and goes back to its languid slumbering.

At the stream, the singer laughs.

"That misplaced self-assurance is going to cost you, as it always does!"

Stepping down from the boulder, he heads toward the village where souls sleep on, blissfully unaware that a *storm* is brewing over their community.

Arriving back in the settlement, he begins walking around every building and along every path, singing as he goes.

His beautiful song flows out, weaving through nooks and crannies, flowing under doors and eaves, dancing up and down loft ladders, anywhere and everywhere. The lovely notes sparkle and shine in the moonlight, in the way that dust motes dance and wink in a beam of sunshine.

Near the water trough, he leans down and draws in the dirt with his finger. To anyone else, his drawings would have appeared to be meaningless lines and squiggles. However, they are not. The drawings are words. Words, which reflect the *new* song he is singing a song consisting of seven notes and seven pure colors: red, orange, yellow, green, blue, indigo, and violet.

The Teacher's wife tosses and turns in the prison room of the Great House. The timber floor is not conducive to a good night's sleep.

Something catches her attention, and she sits up, listening intently. *Is that someone singing?* She stands up. The singing sounds very close. So close in fact, that the Teacher's wife turns, half expecting to see the singer in the room behind her. All she sees, however, is a shifting play of moonlight and shadows.

Shrugging, she curls up on the floor once more. The lovely singing is strangely soothing, and it isn't long before she is sleeping soundly.

Within the shifting moonlight and shadows, there is a smile.

Chapter 12

"My Divine right."

The next day arrives in all its splendor, lighting the tips of the trees and painting the plateau in varying shades of gold.

The Teacher is preparing for the day. However, he desperately wants to know what has happened to his wife. His son keeps asking where his mother is, which doesn't help the Teacher's feelings of guilt. He fobs the boy off with some feeble excuse, while quietly praying that his wife will be released. *Not that he holds any hope.*

In the Great House, the day has gotten off to a more positive beginning. The Code Keeper wakes up feeling refreshed. He had thought he would have a restless night. However, he slept well, like a fox after a productive visit to the chicken house.

After a bracing wash, no breakfast (he is fasting), he puts on his wrinkled trousers and shirt and strides to his office. *There is nothing like a good dose of the Code to start one's day!*

The Keeper decides that the strange experience of the night before was all in his head. The pain of his headache was at fault. He is glad that the Stalwarts or the Healer had not seen him in his state of panic. It would have been damaging to his pride, to say the least.

The Keeper sits down at his desk and opens the timeworn Copy. As he gazes down at the written texts, he wishes it was the *original* Code, the Founder's black leather covered book.

To have *that* book, would be truly inspiring. However, that will never be.

Realizing he must be sounding ungrateful, he quickly apologizes to Divine Providence, thanking the holy Authority for the Copy, and the Divine Agents who wrote it.

The Keeper emits a wistful sigh and stares at the ceiling, pondering *Divine Agents*.

No other Code Keeper ever received a visit from Divine Agents, as far as he is aware. Perhaps they had not measured up. The Code Keeper considers his pious life, mentally ticking off his qualifying points.

He was born a Code Keeper.

His loyalty to the Code is beyond question.

He is not slack in applying discipline and punishment.

He maintains the laws and standards set by the Founder.

He has kept himself pure in every way.

He is above reproach, and he lives out his days in silent contemplation and study of the Code. (When he is not tending to other duties, that is.)

So why is it that a Divine Agent has not yet made an appearance to *him*?

There is no question that he would *not* recognize one. Being a Code Keeper, he would *know* a Divine Agent as soon as he saw one.

"So where are you?" the Keeper snaps peevishly, looking upwards. "If any Code Keeper has earned a visit, it is me! I hereby claim a visit, as my Divine right!"

High on a rocky crag, a cloaked figure throws back his head and lets out a hoot of laughter, startling his companion, the eagle.

"Would you listen to *that*? What do *you* think?"

The eagle bobs its head in a comical way, clicks its beak, screeches, and releases a gob of dropping.

The figure laughs.

"That's one way of putting it."

His face becomes serious. What the Code Keeper wants, is something that cannot be *earned*. There are no *qualifying* factors. He reveals himself to whomever he chooses; in his own way and in his own time. It has nothing to do with the will of men.

The eagle does a shuffle and lets out another ear-splitting screech, followed by sharp *chittering*.

The eagle's companion roars with laughter.

"Hmm, not one for subtlety, are you! I don't think I'll repeat that."

Chapter 13

"Apple blossom?"

The Code Keeper is busy scribbling down notes for his next sermon, unaware of the musings of the two figures on the ridge. The subject of his message is going to be: the evils of music and the devilish lure of *singing*.

His elbow accidentally knocks the horsewhip off the desk and onto the floor. The Keeper smiles as he sets *Righteousness* back on the desktop. Running his fingers over the silver handle he marvels. *The weapon of spiritual warfare! How well it disciplines and shapes unruly souls.*

There is a sharp rap on the door, and one of the Stalwarts pokes his head into the room. He asks the Keeper for instructions regarding the Teacher's wife.

Oddly, the Keeper cannot remember why she is in the Great House. He decides not to waste time on the matter. When he remembers her crime, he'll deal with it. In the meantime, he orders her release.

The shocked Stalwarts head to the cell. Since when have Code Keepers been given to releasing people?

Unable to figure it out, they just do what they have been ordered to do. *Thinking* isn't part of their duties.

The Teacher's wife wakes to the sound of the door bolts rasping. *It's time.* She stands up, smoothing down her skirts.

The Stalwarts enter the cell, expecting to find tears and pleas for mercy. However, none of these things occur. Why isn't she making a fuss?

The Teacher's wife is just as baffled as they are. However, what confuses her more, is the order to return home.

"You're releasing me?"

Both men nod.

She doesn't need to be told twice and rushes past the Stalwarts, who look at each other in some bewilderment. The woman reeks of apple blossom.

As if that isn't puzzling enough, they hear the sound of singing, hovering in the air like an echo. Both men are surprised by a sharp pain in their hearts, and to their horror, tears well up. *By the Code, what is happening to us?* The Stalwarts hasten away to their duties, complaining about allergies, and the annoying effects of pollen.

The Teacher's wife steps out of the Great House and makes for her home. A group of women, who are standing by the water trough, are shocked when they see her. Those taken to the Great House for a serious crime, are rarely seen again. They watch her run home and go inside.

Some seconds pass before they realize there is nothing else to see. In confusion, they pick up buckets. It doesn't matter whose it is or if it is full or not; they just want to get home. The Code Keeper must be in a strange mood, and if he is, they don't want to be caught *gossiping* at the water trough.

The street returns to its empty state.

The Teacher and his son are eating breakfast. They both stare when she walks in, as chirpy as a meadowlark. The Teacher doesn't know what to say.

As she joins them at the table, he notices a sweet fragrance about her. *Apple blossom?*

Questions jostle for attention in the Teacher's head. *The Code Keeper has released her. He must have his reasons for doing so, still...*

Chapter 14

Dreams, Colors, and Beelzebub

The tall figure stands on a jagged peak, his arms spread wide and his long cloak flowing about him.

A small zephyr sweeps up, surrounding him with its soft songs and sighs. He joins in, adding delicate harmonies to the gentle music.

In the Animal yards, ears come alert, listening.

Men working outside feel a sense of something in the air.

Those inside buildings gaze out of windows at the high peaks around them. None of them knows why.

On the peak, the singer grins, then he bursts into laughter—laughter that rolls through the heavens, causing cosmic creations to flare, hum, spin, and dance, in vivid displays of color, and exuberant sound.

Still laughing, he turns his attention to the village below and even though they will not hear him, he shouts: "Look up, people. Look up! Your deliverance is on its way...and it is coming on a Song!"

In the bland homes of the people of the Code, there are startled gasps, widened eyes, smothered exclamations, and quickly hidden smiles.

Color and music are making their presence known in small, unassuming ways: bright berries snagged in a headscarf or flowers caught up in an armful of firewood; apples gleaming red in the light of candles, or swirling colors in a drop of oil.

Small, insignificant ways, yet the people are *noticing*.

"What's wrong with color?" cries one young man to his father. "Color surrounds us. If Divine Providence created everything, then it seems to me that Divine Providence enjoys color very much!"

His father gives him a hearty smack on the back of the head for speaking disrespectfully.

"Divine Providence does not *enjoy* anything. Divine Providence is holy! Too holy for such nonsense."

The boy wanders off, muttering to himself while rubbing the back of his head.

As for the Teacher's wife: a spring of joy is bubbling away inside, like the dancing, bubbling waters of a mountain stream. Life has gained a sparkle, and all she wants to do is sing! Why? She has no explanation.

In another home, the daughter of one of the Hunters is waking up with songs on *her* lips. She quickly stifles them before her parents hear. She is old enough to know that she cannot afford to start singing out loud. *Maybe sometime in the future?*

The Tailor has noticed a new sparkle in his wife's eyes. He hears her humming happy tunes when she thinks he's not around. Secretly enjoying the sound, the Tailor decides not to say anything. Perhaps he will try it himself. *It would be one way to kick back against their ridiculous laws and rules.* The thought brings a huge smile to his face.

The Grower's wife has been having pleasant dreams of brightly colored skirts and shawls. Every morning she looks at her dull hemp clothing and wants to scream. Perhaps they'll be able to wear beautiful colors one day? Who knows? *It's possible, isn't it?*

Many children are whispering about dreams. In these dreams, they are walking through flower-covered fields, under bright blue skies. There are streams of rainbow-colored water and birds are singing. A tall person walks with them.

The children wish they could go there, because it's a "happy" place, and they like the "happy" person in the dream. The mothers have never heard the word "happy" used so much in their lives.

The Teacher himself has dreamed.

In his dream, he is sitting on a rock, talking with someone in a robe of many colors. They are gazing over a small lake, the far side lush with trees and flowering undergrowth. A small waterfall sings as it flows into the lake. The scene is peaceful and serene.

The Teacher asks the man questions, and the man gives him answers, answers which soothe his heart and fill him with peace.

When the Teacher wakes up, he is full of both longing and disappointment. Longing to know such a person and disappointment that he never will. *After all, it was only a dream.*

Throughout the village, dreams, visions, and awakenings are occurring in every heart that is hungry and yearning for life.

However, for the individuals in the Great House, there are no dreams, visions, or awakenings. They are content with their work and content with their positions of importance. There is no hunger or yearning for better things. They like things just as they are.

The only thing they *are* aware of is a subtle change in the emotional makeup of the community, similar to a shift in the wind.

The Code Keeper, ever vigilant in the monitoring of his flock, is on high alert.

As the weeks pass, he concludes that *something* is influencing the community. The people are restless and becoming more easily distracted.

The Keeper casts his mind back, looking for a point of reference from which the subtle changes began. It doesn't take him long to find it—*the stranger!*

The Keeper's concern deepens, and he wonders if the man's singing had woven some spell.

Rattled, he decides to assemble the people and warn them about the evils of *distractions* and the wiles of the devil.

As soon as the people have gathered in the Assembly field, the Code Keeper launches into his sermon. As usual, he plows straight in. He doesn't believe in messing about.

"I've noticed that many of you are slipping into daydreaming and distractions. Be warned! Stay alert! Distractions are from the Evil One. Those who allow themselves to be ensnared by distractions will be severely disciplined!"

The Keeper opens his mouth to deliver another volley. However, something catches his eye. It is a chestnut colt prancing in the nearby coral. Struck by the beauty of the horse's movements, he lapses into silence.

The people notice and are both amused and afraid. Amused, because their illustrious leader has himself fallen into a *distraction*, and scared because *they* will be the ones to suffer for it.

The Stalwarts and Healer catch each other's eyes. One of them gives a loud, deliberate cough. At the sound, the Code Keeper snaps back to attention. Realizing what has happened, he gives vent to a tree-felling roar.

"Beelzebub! It's the workings of Beelzebub!"

"Of course it's *Beelzebub*," someone in the crowd sighs. "If it isn't our fault, it's *his*. What Code Keeper ever admits to a fault, for *anything*."

Deaf to the soft murmurings here and there, the Code Keeper continues.

"You see how cunning the enemy is? You see? Even *I* need to be on guard, and I am the most sanctified of you all."

One or two of the men cough loudly to hide unbidden snorts of laughter. The Stalwarts glare about, looking for the guilty parties. The culprits turn a delicate shade of blue as they choke themselves into silence.

The Code Keeper dismisses the people, adding final warnings about *Beelzebub* and tossing in threats of punishment if they don't focus on their tasks.

He then storms back to the Great House, muttering about the "machinations" of *Beelzebub,* and the "devilish distraction" of prancing horses.

The Healer and Stalwarts follow, avoiding each other's eyes while trying to keep straight faces.

As the people return to their tasks, many of the women wonder what the Keeper's reaction would be, if he knew what *they* get up to in the evenings. If a prancing horse can get him *that* worked up, their special *moments* would probably send the Keeper into an apoplectic fit, strong enough to finish him off permanently!

"If only..." some of the women mutter to themselves, tongue in cheek.

As soon as their evening duties have been taken care of, and children in bed, wives, and mothers bundle themselves up and head outside. They stand or sit, behind their homes, gazing up toward the night-shrouded slopes.

When husbands question them about their nocturnal activity, they give a variety of answers, covering everything from "meditating" to "thanking the Code" for their godly menfolk. The husbands accept whatever the women tell them. As long as the women are quiet, and don't stray far from the house, there is no reason for the men to be concerned.

So, while husbands doze by the fire, secure in the arms of their egos, their wives sit outside, waiting.

It usually isn't long before a melody of indescribable loveliness, drifts down to them, from the surrounding slopes. The gentle song flows around the women, wrapping them in its beautiful embrace. They close their eyes, letting the soft music paint bright and happy scenes. In the case of the Teacher's wife, the song conjures up tantalizing images of beautifully baked bread! *If only.*

The lovely melody soothes troubled minds and quietens agitated hearts. It is only a song. However, the women love it. They draw pleasure, strength, and delight from it.

When the song finally ebbs away, the women sit quietly for a moment before (with no small amount of reluctance) going back indoors.

Alone in their narrow cot beds in the lofts, the women smile secret smiles and curl up with the glow of the strange music warming their aching, lonely hearts, and sometimes (unfortunately for some), aching, hurting bodies.

Those who suffer the latter can't help wondering if their predecessors had to put up with similar.

CHAPTER 15

A Nightmare Journey.

Pope's followers were fed up. Where were the blessings Pope had promised them?

Day in and day out, they were forced to endure his fiery visions, ecstatic pronouncements, and the endless preaching from his black book, the Code.

The journey was a nightmare.

Problems weren't coming in twos or threes; they were coming in droves.

Pope was the biggest problem of all. He drove them harder than he drove his horses!

As they journeyed, Pope would ride off now and again, for varying lengths of time. When he returned, he would often have one or two livestock in tow. Or items he believed would be beneficial to their new community.

"Divine provision!" Pope would announce to the people.

(The truth was, Pope had hidden his wealth in small caches in his wagon. Heading toward a new Destiny hadn't included abandoning the contents of the family vault. A little detail, the people, didn't need to know.)

Seasons came and went. The travelers endured the heat and sweat of summer and the bone-cracking cold of winter.

On the rare occasions that death occurred, due to mishap or illness, burials were tended to very quickly. Not even death was permitted to slow down their progress.

Their zealous leader regarded the arduous journey as a sifting process, a *refining*. The journey was going to separate 'goats' from 'sheep,' and 'dross' from 'gold.'

Anything that Pope regarded as *sin*, was dealt with by *Righteousness*. According to Pope, discipline led to *sanctification*. He constantly let his followers know that there was a great deal of 'sanctifying' work to be done before they could reap the blessings and rewards.

Righteousness had a busy time of it.

Pope maintained an aloofness from his followers. He was not there to be anybody's friend. He was there to fulfill a holy Calling, and that was it. He was *appointed* and *anointed*. They were not. *He* was the representative of the Divine, while they were...?

When his followers encountered difficulties, Pope offered no help, nor would he permit others to render assistance. It was all part of the refining process. In other words: deal with it and move on, or don't deal with it and be left behind.

One or two souls, unable to tolerate conditions (and Pope) any longer, stole away in the dark hours of the night and were never seen again.

Pope wasn't concerned. He declared that such individuals were not needed, and they were all better off without them.

Depressed and beaten down, his followers struggled on, clinging to Pope's promises of blessings, in the same way, that limpets cling to the bottom of a ship.

The day came when they found themselves in a vast mountain range, that stretched north and south as far as the eye could see.

To the people, the steep forested slopes represented more exhausting challenges. They hoped Pope would lead them in another direction.

Pope, however, was taking a keen interest in the area. There was *something* about it.

Scouts were sent to investigate. Pope and the rest of the people made camp while they waited for the scouts' return.

The following day, the weary scouts plodded into camp. Pope listened in silence as they relayed to him what they had found. They described a long steep climb and a vast plateau surrounded on three sides by a high escarpment.

A hidden plateau? Pope felt stirrings of excitement.

The scouts warned him that if he intended going to the plateau, they would have to dispense with the wagons, or at least dismantle them. They also warned him that the climb would be tough and some might not be able to make it. The scouts knew how tired the people were. The young ones would be okay. However, the older folk might not.

Pope had heard all he wanted to hear.

His mind was already made up.

He ordered the men to get some rest. Preparations would begin early the next morning.

As soon as it was light, Pope rounded the people up and gave them new orders. They were going to do the climb. Many hearts quailed as they gazed up at the thickly forested slope. It seemed impossible.

The tired, worn-out wagons were emptied and dismantled. What was too large or bulky got abandoned. Pope ordered those pieces burnt. The ashes and remains, scattered. Some wondered about this. It was as if Pope didn't want any *evidence* left behind.

Pope ordered that pieces which could serve some purpose, be carried by cattle or horses. Other items, he arranged to be dragged behind on roughly assembled sleds. Those given this particular task groaned and wondered for the millionth time, why they hadn't headed south instead of following after Pope.

It took some time to get everything prepared and ready, but finally, the moment arrived. Pope gave the order for them to begin the daunting climb.

Step by step and in agonizing slowness, the people fought their way up through the forest, hauling and dragging goods and supplies with them, while others toiled hard, pushing and pulling livestock.

It was a nightmare climb. Some souls reached the limit of their endurance and fell to one side, promising they would get up and follow when they could.

Progress was so slow that Pope soon saw the wisdom of allowing the people to rest where they were. It would be foolish to stumble up through the forest in the dark, with only a few torches to guide them. There were too many of them, plus animals.

Guards were posted to watch for any signs of bears, mountain lions or wolves. Thankfully the night hours passed without any threat or mishap.

As soon as Pope saw the first hint of sunlight, the people were ordered up, and the climb began again. Nobody had been lost, and amazingly, the animals were still with them. Pope deemed it a "miracle."

At last, the people dragged themselves and their loads, out from the forest shadows and onto the vast plateau. Exhausted, they sat in the lush meadow grass, looking at the amazing scene around them, while livestock and horses fell to grazing.

It was just as the scouts had said: a vast grassy plateau stretching far to the left and right, surrounded by a high escarpment of jagged peaks and ridgelines. A natural amphitheater.

Pope, scanned the area for some minutes then turned to his drooping followers and grandly announced that their journey was over.

Here would be the home of the Chosen.

Here would be the life of blessing, as promised.

The people emitted great sighs of relief. Their journey had come to an end, and now they could rest.

Many fell back in the fragrant grass and closed their eyes. Very soon the mountain air was filled with the sound of heavy breathing and scattered snoring.

Pope's angry shouts, jerked the sleepers awake.

There was to be no sleeping!

Pope had been planning and preparing throughout the entire journey. He wasn't going to let any "sluggardly" followers ruin his *moment*.

While the bone-weary people struggled to stay awake, Pope revealed the foundational rules and laws that were going to govern their new settlement and their lives.

As the people listened, they became more and more dejected. Pope's interpretation of a *blessed* life, was entirely different to theirs!

Chapter 16

Fierce Confrontation

In the high mountain community of the Chosen, it is another pleasant day. Not too hot and not too cold. In other words, an average kind of day.

The men are at their workstations and students are learning arithmetic in the school. The leaders are busy in their Great House and families are quietly occupying themselves in their homes.

None of them is aware that the stranger has returned.

After seating himself on the stone wall of the water trough, as he did before, the stranger launches into a bright, happy song. The merry tune skips and dances through the air, straight into the ears of the women and children, busy in their homes.

The women try to ignore the sound by thinking of angry husbands, skinning rabbits, washing floors, anything. However, it is no use. Their feet are tapping, and they find themselves humming. Delighted children are laughing and clapping in response.

The Teacher's wife is in the middle of washing the floor. When she hears his singing, she drops the cloth, and dashes to the door, tripping over the wooden bucket in her hurry.

Women and young ones pour into the street, drawn by the stranger's happy song. One little boy, excited by the singing, runs on chubby legs, straight up to the stranger. Seeing the little fellow's delight, the stranger scoops him up and begins tossing him into the air. The little boy laughs and chortles while his mother looks on, smiling. The other children hold back at first, but when they see their little friend playing with the stranger's cloak and pulling at his hair, they forget their shyness. They cluster around him, chattering away like a flock of noisy sparrows.

The singer laughs, enjoying being surrounded by happy children. Standing up, he leads them in a merry dance up and down the street.

Stalwarts, Keepers, and Healers are completely forgotten.

The singer's heart is overflowing. These little ones are enjoying him in a way that many who claim long relationship with him, have never known, and may never know, being unable (or unwilling) to see beyond their narrow, rigid perceptions of him.

He smiles down at the laughing, happy crowd. *All of my children should be like this, no matter who they are or how old.*

A furious roar shatters the air. The Keeper has stepped out of the building for a breath of fresh air and discovered the happy *festivity* in the street.

Everyone scatters, like terrified chickens. Mothers scoop up little ones and young folk duck and weave in their mad dash home.

The singer waits quietly by the water trough; his face is expressionless.

The Code Keeper storms toward the stranger, in long angry strides. He cannot believe that the man has had the gall to return and what's worse, has led the women and children in sinful behavior.

"How dare you!" he bellows with every step. "Who do you think you are, that you come into *my* village, bringing this evil and wickedness with you?"

Behind him, the Healer and Stalwarts come running, horsewhips in their hands.

The stranger sighs. *Nothing has changed. Not since man first grasped power to himself and used it to kill his br*other.

The enraged Code Keeper jabs the stranger in the chest with the silver handle of *Righteousness*.

"How dare you lead the women and children in ungodly behavior? They are *my* people, and *I* will not allow your *evil* to corrupt their lives."

Blue-green eyes look deep into the Code Keeper's angry ones. Although the stranger's lips do not move, the Keeper distinctly hears himself addressed.

"Your people, Code Keeper? I think not! They belong to the Father of Lights. Not you, or any other man!"

The words cut deep, like a two-edged sword. The Code Keeper takes several steps backward. *Why does this voice sound familiar?*

The *Other* jerks awake, shocked that the enemy has slipped through its defenses. It leaps into action, flooding the Code Keeper with a rancid song of attack.

The Keeper snarls in the stranger's face, unaware that another is using him.

"Who do you think you are? *I* am the one with authority. *I* am the one with the power. These are *my* people, and it is *my* will that..."

"Aren't you tired of singing that same old song?"

The words, spoken directly to the *Other*, impact it like a resounding slap in the face.

In white-hot fury, the *Other* lashes out through one of the Stalwarts—the man delivers a stinging blow to the stranger's face.

Those piercing blue-green eyes turn toward the Stalwart, who stumbles back, his heart thudding strangely.

The music of the *Other*, thrums loudly within the Keeper, driving him mercilessly. The Code Keeper lets loose a string of invectives.

The Stalwarts are shocked by what is coming out of the Code Keeper's mouth. They've never heard such words before. *Where are they coming from?*

The Keeper jams the silver handle of *Righteousness*, up under the stranger's jaw, and in soft, menacing tones, he hisses, "Whoever you are and *whatever* you are, you will not violate this community one second longer."

Turning to the Stalwarts, the Keeper snarls, "You *know* where to take him."

Yes, they know, only too well.

Loathe for actual contact; the Stalwarts use their whip handles to prod the stranger forward. To their surprise, he does not resist.

(The *Other* smiles maliciously. Now, *this* is more like it.)

The men have heard the shouts of the Code Keeper from their workstations. Downing tools, they approach the scene. In the schoolhouse, the eldest boys take charge.

The gathered men are unsure what to do. Should they follow their leaders or should they stay put? Usually, only Elders accompany Code Keepers to the Tree.

Doubts assail a few. What has the stranger done to deserve *this* punishment?

Hearing their doubts, the *Other* sings a malodorous song through their souls.

"Yesss...take him to the Tree. He is a threat. He has to go. The Tree will fix things..."

As the toxic song takes effect, the men find themselves nodding in agreement. They set out after their leaders, hands resting on the ugly horsewhips attached to their leather belts.

CHAPTER 17

"Sing!"

The Animal Keeper is in one of the pens of the Animal yards. He is about to dispatch a lamb for the needs of the Great House when he sees the procession of men approaching. He notes the stranger among them and sighs. *Another victim for the Tree.*

As the men draw level with the pen, the stranger turns his head. Blue-green eyes gaze directly into the Animal Keeper's own, rooting him to the spot. The stranger turns his head away, and the spell breaks.

Shaking his head, the Animal Keeper turns to complete his task, however, as he readies the knife, the lamb looks up. The Animal Keeper gasps and reels back. For a split second, he'd been staring into those blue-green eyes again. *How could that be?* With a surge of anger toward the lamb, which he is at a loss to explain, he completes his bloody task.

The procession winds its way along the plateau, then branches off and begins climbing a steep, narrow trail, up the escarpment slopes.

A purple-black cloud is spreading across the sky like an ugly bruise, and the men turn up the collars of their coats. It looks like a storm is developing. They hope that once they get to the Tree, the punishment will be swift. None of them wants to be caught out on the steep slopes in a raging storm.

None of the men are aware that down on the plateau, somebody has followed them.

With courage she didn't know she possessed, the Teacher's wife has ventured out onto the trail. Some distance from the village she stops. Angry looking clouds are rapidly spreading across the sky, like ink spreading through water. Lightning flashes and thunder rolls. A fierce wind is approaching, whipping the tops of the trees and flattening crops.

The Teacher's wife hesitates, wondering if she should go back to the village. Too late! The storm is upon her, blowing dust and grit everywhere. Her face stings and she covers her eyes to protect them from the flying dust.

The storm is ferocious. With every crash and roll of thunder, the ground trembles. Lightning flashes and flickers all around. In the middle of the raging elements, the Teachers wife has only one concern—the stranger! *What is happening to him? Is he suffering already?*

In her mind, she sees him being led away like a lamb to the slaughter, and she bursts into tears.

He'd brought no threat with him. All he'd brought was his beautiful singing.

She rails at herself, angry that none of them had found the courage to help him. They had all turned tail and run, leaving him at the mercy of their heartless leaders.

Her anger becomes despair. What can a mere housewife do anyway? If the men can't stand up against their tyrannical leaders, what hope does *she* have? Feeling helpless and useless, she turns back toward the village.

The wind suddenly drops. Everything becomes still, and there is an eerie silence.

"Sing!"

The Teacher's wife looks around, hearing the word but seeing nobody.

"Sing!"

Fear creeps in.
"Don't be afraid."
"Who are you? Why do you want me to sing?"
"SING!"
The word rings with *authority.*
Feeling foolish, the Teacher's wife starts to sing.

Her song has no pattern or structure; she sings whatever comes into her mind, letting melodies come as they will.

The wind suddenly picks up again. It is howling with a new ferocity, for the *Other* is hiding within the wind, adding its rage to the violent gusts.

Preoccupied with driving the men along on their hate-filled mission, the *Other* had not noticed the woman's presence on the path. However, when her singing penetrated its awareness, the *Other* raced to silence her. It had detected something *more* coming through her songs.

From within the wind, the *Other* screams abuse. It batters the Teacher's wife with hatred, slams her with spite, and pummels her with evil purpose.

The Teacher's wife keeps singing, despite the furious onslaught.

Something extraordinary now occurs.

A *new* song surges up; a song that is way beyond her capabilities. The song is powerful; one that will brook no challenge. It punches into the face of the wind, driving the *Other* back.

The Teacher's wife marvels. She knows that the song is not hers. It is coming from somewhere else. She guesses that it is coming from the new music within her. As she abandons herself to the Song, she feels infused with energy, as if a fast-flowing river is surging through her.

The powerful song rings out, Authority and Declaration in its tones. She can hear this, even though she does not understand the words for she is singing in a strange language. The Teacher's wife is surprised, but not alarmed. The beautiful words curl and dance on her tongue in rhythmic cadences, reminding her of the drumming sound of galloping horses.

The *Other* seethes. It loathes the new song with every fiber of its being, for it knows whose song it is, and knows the message contained within it.

In a violent rage, the *Other* hurls itself against the woman, trying desperately to silence her. However, its efforts are useless and the *Other* screams in impotent rage.

In the Beginning, it thought it had won—broken the Plan, ruined the Dream. However, as it watched events unfolding through the ages, understanding had dawned. While it had been caught up plotting and scheming, believing in its indomitable cunning and voracity, Victory had been determined, signed, sealed and delivered through *Him*!

How had it not known? It had been Guardian of the Glory. It had been right there yet it *had not seen what was coming!*

Since that awful revelation, hatred consumes it, burning like a continual, tormenting fire. Already defeated, all it can do is play out its hate, weaving its music into as many souls as it can, so that when its end comes, it will not be alone.

The *Other* turns a cold, vengeful eye upon the woman on the path.

Puny humanity! What is so appealing about *them* that they matter? They are nothing! They don't even acknowledge the One who made them.

What glory do they have? What power? They have none! *They* have never stood in the source of Light, radiating Splendor. *They* have never filled the heavens with the sounds of their pipes and flutes. *What music it made! What glory it created...*

"*What pride!*"

The *Other* flinches. It knows who has spoken.

Now the *Other* turns surly.

"*I may be beaten, but I can still inflict pain on you by inflicting pain on them!*"

The enemy of souls moves to strike the young woman but in that instant, there is a deafening '*CRACK,*' and the whole world turns blinding, searing white.

After a few moments, the Teacher's wife sits up. She'd thought her end had come when the lightning bolt struck. Despite being hurled to the ground, her only injury (of sorts) is ringing in her ears and a few spots before her eyes.

The powerful strike has left an area of the field blackened, and the crops in it destroyed.

The Teacher's wife looks around her. Red-gold light tips the ridgeline and the shadows are long. The storm clouds have dispersed. As for the wind—all she can hear is its whimpering sigh as it limps away across the fields...defeated.

It's time to go home. There is spilled water to clean up, (not to mention herself), and the evening meal to prepare.

As soon as she is back in her home, she ponders the event on the path.

What happened is beyond her understanding but not beyond her comprehension. She knows that there was far more going on in that storm than was natural. Something had been raging against her. However, a greater force had risen and turned her feeble singing into something powerful. Whatever the battle had been about, victory was accomplished.

"We won," she shouts, her hands punching skyward. "We stood against it, we sang, and we won!"

She spins around in a burst of wild exuberance, laughing and singing, her hands alternately clapping and lifting heavenward.

The Teacher's wife is ecstatic. Exciting things are happening: the stranger, his singing, dancing, battles, and music in her heart.

Chapter 18

Desperation and a Dream

The men are back from their journey to the Tree.

They have torn clothing, scratches, cuts, and bruises. Naturally, the women are curious. However, the men refuse to talk. After cleaning themselves up and tending to their injuries in silence, the men retire to their beds.

None of them can sleep.

The incident at the Tree revealed that they are woefully ignorant of many things. The only knowledge they have is that which is dispensed out to them by Code Keepers, in the same way, a Healer dispenses herbal remedies. *What if there is more to life than they have been led to believe?* Troubled and in some distress, the men toss and turn, desperately hoping that sleep will bring them a measure of peace.

The Teacher arrives home with *his* thoughts and fears bubbling away like water in a pot. Scared and confused, he falls into his coping mechanism—anger, and he knows exactly where to direct it.

Storming into his home, he comes to a halt opposite his wife who has been sitting up, waiting for him.

Full of anger, he doesn't notice the light of joy on her face. All he sees is a target.

Pointing a shaking finger at her, the Teacher snarls, "You! I don't know how, but I *know* you are to blame!"

She stares at his wild appearance; the torn clothing and the scratches on his face and arms.

"You have brought all this upon us. You stole what is forbidden and hid it in our home! Everything that is happening is *your* fault!"

She is stunned by his outburst. Her heart feels like it has been kicked by a mule and her newfound happiness runs, cowering in a corner.

The Teacher hasn't finished his rant.

"You are different, ever since you returned from the Great House. There is something (he searched for the right word)— *extra* in you. The Code Keeper should have punished you. He *should* have driven you out."

For a few moments, there is only the sound of his ragged breathing; then a strange look slides across his face.

"What *witchcraft* did you engage in, to escape punishment?"

There is silence for a moment then, with a loud scrape of her chair, his wife stands up, her face flushing red.

"There was no *witchcraft,* and you know it. Your anger is blinding you, as it usually does. Perhaps the Keeper simply had a change of heart?"

He stabs a finger toward her.

"A change of heart? Never! He honors the Code, which *clearly* states...."

Her voice cuts like a knife.

"You men and your Code. I *hate* the Code. I've had enough of it! You use the wretched texts to justify beatings and punishment. Are *these* the blessings promised by the Founder? And just *who* was the Founder anyway? Another blind, arrogant man, like the rest of you?"

The Teacher cannot believe his ears. His entire face turns crimson.

"Blasphemy!" he roars, his whole body trembling. "You have gone too far!"

He snatches at the horsewhip, attached to his belt, however as he does, an alien thought rips through his mind.

"Have a care..."

He shakes his head to remove the treacherous thought and continues detaching the horsewhip.

"You know what she has suffered."

For a moment he hesitates, however, pride, anger, and pig-headed stubbornness, make him release the horsewhip from its fastening.

"Remember..."

An image of his father unexpectedly fills his mind, followed by memories of beatings, and his father's endless lecturing.

The Teacher slams the table with his horsewhip. *Enough!* Is he not the head of his house? Is he not the authority in his home? His wife needs disciplining, and by the Code, he will not let sentiment stand in his way.

Shaking off the memories and the niggling voice, he steps toward her.

His wife sees the determination on his face. At first, she shrinks back, then, from somewhere deep, courage surges up. Her hands ball into fists.

"You will NOT!"

The last word slams the Teacher in the face. For a second he is stunned, speechless, then his eyes widen. In two strides he is around the table. Grabbing his wife he shakes her while shouting, "You do *not* tell *me* what to do!"

"Hurt me, and you also hurt your unborn child."

He hears her words and freezes.

"What did you say?"

"You heard me," she replies, looking him straight in the eyes.

Tense moments pass as the two of them glare at each other like combatants, then with an angry expletive, the Teacher lets her go. In a flash of temper, he flings the horsewhip across the room, pulls out a chair and thumps down into it.

He dares not punish her now.

The birth of a second child, especially a girl, will mean his elevation to that of an *Elder*; a status which accords more honor.

His wife can see that her husband is musing on his future rise in status and shakes her head. One would think it was the *man* who carried the child, went through the rigors of birth, then raised and cared for it. *They get the honors, while we women get the work…and the lashings!*

Her thoughts are interrupted by their son who is calling from the loft. He's been woken up by all the noise. She asks permission to go and tend to him.

The Teacher nods absent-mindedly.

On trembling legs, his wife mounts the dark stairs.

The danger is past. *For now.*

Downstairs, the Teacher is trying to bring some order into his chaotic thoughts.

Not only does he have the incident on the mountain to deal with, he now has an openly rebellious wife. In addition to all of that, she is pregnant! This is excellent news but on top of everything else…?

He thumps the table. *How is a man expected to cope?*

Wearily, he gets to his feet.

There's an important task to be done in the morning. He'd better get some sleep while he can. It's been an exhausting and eventful day.

After a quick wash, he falls into his bed by the fire and is soon snoring.

Upstairs in the loft, his wife curls up in her bedcovers. She wonders what happened on the mountain, and why her husband came home in such a state. Her thoughts turn to the stranger. He came into their village like a ray of light, giving them a glimpse of how life *could* be. *If only...?*

With tears in her eyes, she burrows under the covers. Sleep quickly enfolds her.

The Teacher's wife dreams.

In her dream, a tall figure in a long cloak of shifting lights and shadows draws near and speaks to her.

"Don't be afraid. All will be well."

The beautiful cloak envelops her, and she feels lifted up as if on great wings. Together they soar into the glittering night skies.

Below her, she sees a blue-green orb, and she asks her companion about it.

His voice is gentle.

"It is Earth."

In her dream, she sighs.

"...so beautiful."

Love resonates in her companion's softly spoken response.

"She is, isn't she—the loveliest of them all."

In her dream, the Teacher's wife gazes around the high dome of the heavens. Her heart thrills at the glorious display of shimmering, sparkling lights. As she gazes in awe at the innumerable jewels and gems aglow in the vast velvet canopy, she suddenly gives a start. *There is sound in the heavens?*

Her companion laughs, and his laughter is musical.

"Did you think the heavens were silent? Listen..."

Sounds are flowing, roaring, surging in all directions like fast-moving rivers. Some of the rushing torrents are entwining, spiraling together at tremendous speed. Others crash together, their powerful impact sending thrumming vibrations and turbulent cracklings of energy racing away through the glittering vastness.

She puts her hands over her ears.

"It's so noisy!"

His happy laughter rings out.

"Yes, it is. The heavens love to sing, as do I."

He immediately bursts into song.

She can feel Power humming through him, and sees colors and light radiating outward in great waves. With every breath of his mouth, miracles take place: bright galaxies blaze into life, singing in strange tones; objects glow in vibrant colors, tapping out staccato rhythms as they spin. Heavenly spheres burst into life in blinding explosions of light, and beautiful nebulas sparkle with bright colors while singing in harmonic cadences.[4]

The heavens are singing, and their songs are jubilant.

Something within her awakens.

In a timid voice, her *spirit* asks, *"Do I know you? Have we met before?"*

The whisper that comes in swift response is as soft and gentle as a lover's kiss.

"I once sang with you in a garden."

Her spirit ponders and memories stir. *A garden?*

Memory trembles.

Joy—Pain—Separation followed by searching, and a yearning for...?

Light dawns.

"It's You!"

Like a child snuggling into the arms of its mother, her spirit nestles into the embracing arms of Love and Light.

"Welcome Home," Love whispers. "Welcome Home!"

CHAPTER 19

Reluctant Messenger

As the Teacher is finishing his breakfast the next morning, he casts furtive looks at his wife. There is a radiance in her that is more than the glow of pregnancy. *Yes, there's something different.* He wonders what is causing it.

The Teacher's wife *is* happy. She woke up feeling *fantastic!* The confrontation of the night before and the hurt she felt at his accusations have been washed away in a most remarkable sense of *well-being.* What has brought about this wonderful change?

She feels as if the answer is dancing along the edges of her mind. It comes tantalizingly close but skips away when she tries to grab on to it. *Was it a dream? A dream of lights and shadows?*

She decides to let it go. Dreams have a way of revealing themselves if and when they feel like it.

The Teacher dawdles over his breakfast, his thoughts lazily jumping from one thing to another. They inevitably turn to the previous evening's confrontation with his wife.

He recaptures his wife's anger; the way her eyes flashed and her cheeks flushed. She's never stood up to him before. It was quite an experience. He feels his cheeks grow warm, as he pictures the scene.

The Teacher casts another furtive look at his wife, watching as she ties her apron around her (slender) waist; and how her skirts sway when she moves.

The Teacher falls into a bout of coughing, as he chokes on a spoonful of oatmeal.

Next minute he sits bolt upright and his spoon falls with a clatter. He'd been so distracted by his wife, that for a moment, he'd forgotten everything else: the event at the Tree and the news that has to be passed on!

The Teacher shudders. *I don't envy whoever gets that little task.*

With a last glance at his wife (which leaves his face burning for some inexplicable reason), he leaves for the schoolhouse, his son in tow.

The students are already sitting quietly in the schoolroom when the Teacher arrives.

As he lays out the day's lessons, a group of Elders comes to the schoolhouse, asking that he join them outside.

Those students who can see through the window, note that the Elders look nervous, and the Teacher doesn't look happy.

Finally, the Teacher re-enters the schoolroom.

"The sons of the Keeper, Healer and Stalwarts will accompany us to the Great House. The rest of you do some revision."

These particular young men glance at each other. *What's this about?*

All four of them are the same age, with a bond established between them; a bond that isn't so much one of friendship, as it is a bond of *recognition*; acknowledgment of the roles each of them will play in the future.

Once inside the Meeting room of the Great House, they are asked to sit down.

"Well? What is it?"

The Code Keeper's son knows what his status is, and has no hesitation in speaking up.

The Teacher looks at the other men. However, their only response is a lot of throat clearing and shuffling of feet. None of them will meet his eyes. He sighs deeply. *Trust me to get stuck with the task.*

"An event has transpired which...*necessitates*...the four of you stepping into your roles sooner than expected."

Four pairs of eyes lock onto the Teacher.

"Something unfortunate occurred on the mountain. Your fathers have moved on. We offer our regrets. They served well, but now you must take up the mantles which have fallen to you."

Their minds reel. What is the Teacher saying? They'd noticed that their fathers were absent, but that was nothing unusual.

The Teacher continues.

"You know what your duty is. You have received training since you were young. All of you are of age. Do not fail your fathers or the people of the Code!"

The young men stare at each other. The Teacher is telling them that their fathers are *dead!*

It takes a few moments for the news to sink in. They are old enough, with enough training and education to step up to the task. However, these are *mantles* with significant responsibilities. For a moment, the four young men just want to run back to the schoolhouse and hide in arithmetic and spelling.

As the Code Keeper's son ponders his new role, it dawns on him that he will no longer be on the receiving end of discipline. His father's never-ending tirades and punishments are over! The new Code Keeper almost bursts into tears at the thought. A gleam now comes into his eyes. *He* will be the one doling out discipline.

"Where is *Righteousness*? It's passed from father to son, so it is now mine!"

The Teacher beckons to one of the Elders, who hands over the silver-handled horsewhip with a degree of (understandable) reluctance.

The young man holds the whip in his hands, and a warm glow infuses him. *He* is now the Code Keeper. The young man can't help smiling to himself.

The other three are experiencing similar thoughts. An understanding of the power they will have in their respective roles is dawning upon each of them in rosy hues.

The Teacher has been watching their faces closely. *Oh yes, they are going to be real sons of their fathers.*

The Elders and the Teacher quietly wait. They've delivered the news. The next step is now in the hands of their new leaders.

After a few moments, the new Code Keeper thanks them for bringing the news of their fathers' deaths. He promises that he will be as zealous as his father was, and expresses the hope that he will lead them to even *greater* godliness in the coming years.

(The waiting men groan inwardly.)

The new Keeper lets them know, that at some point, he will be calling on them to reveal every detail of what transpired on the mountain.

The Teacher feels a tingle of concern. The new Keeper's tone sounded ominous.

Chapter 20

"Start strong, stay strong..."

The new Code Keeper is busy going through his father's notes. Putting down the parchments, he leans back in the chair and gazes around the room.

It is stark and functional, with shelves containing bundles of records, books, and jottings. These are the writings of all other Code Keepers, going as far back as the Founder himself.

A flash of panic sears through the young man. Despite *knowing* what his Calling entails, he lacks proper experience. How is he going to cope with it all?

He picks up *Righteousness*, studying the workmanship. The silver handle still has some of the fine detail, engraved by what must have been a very talented silversmith. He runs his fingers over the fine leather strips, woven tightly over a strong central core. It's an excellent piece of artistry and one which has been carefully maintained.

A small shiver runs down the Keeper's spine as he realizes that the Founder's hands have gripped and used the handsome horsewhip. *So many hands have wielded it, and now mine.*

The Code Keeper looks across the room to the wooden board on which several other horsewhips are hanging. These are the ones used for general everyday disciplining. *Righteousness* is more a symbol of their authority and is only used occasionally, out of respect for its age, and the original owner.

An idea hums through his mind.

The Teacher once told them that when faced with a daunting task, the way to cope was to throw oneself into it.

The young man nods to himself.

That's what he will do. *I'll be better than you, father. I'll be the most feared and respected Code Keeper the people have ever known.*

The young Keeper is now feeling a great deal more confident. He remembers what his father used to say: "Start strong, stay strong and finish stronger!"

His thoughts turn momentarily to the Stalwarts and the Healer.

The two new Stalwarts have moved into the Great House. He determines to keep them both busy.

The new Healer has moved into the building next to the Great House. All the herbs and materials of the Healer's trade are there. He has all his father's records, and recipes so he should have no problems doing his job.

The Code Keeper's thoughts turn to recent events.

He knows about the stranger's visit. Thankfully, the problem was dealt with. However, there is the matter of the sinful display on the part of the women and children. Unbelievably, it involved singing and dancing. *Dancing!* Even his sister had been caught up in it. (Not that *that* surprised him.)

He decides that administering a healthy dose of discipline will be an excellent start to his reign. It will send a clear message: that although young for a Code Keeper, he will be rigorous in his duty and will exercise his authority with enthusiasm.

Feeling pleased with himself, he sends out the word that all are to assemble behind the Great House. The people get no warning or time to *prepare*. They are rounded up by the Stalwarts and rushed to the Assembly field.

This is the young Keeper's first assembly, and just as he promised himself, he launches in hard and strong.

"Emotional displays! Forbidden behavior!"

His words ring through the air.

Bodies shuffle and fidget. Shoulders slump.

"Did you think the matter was forgotten?"

He glares out. Nobody meets his gaze.

"You men dealt with the stranger at the Tree. Does anyone have anything to add or say on this?"

The Teacher clears his throat. A Hunter and Carpenter each grab an arm surreptitiously.

(The Teacher had no hesitation in reporting his wife. He could be feeling duty-bound to reveal more about other things.)

"Not yet," they murmur to the Teacher, who knows what they are thinking. His face flushes.

The Code Keeper is still talking, pacing back and forth, his hands behind his back. He turns and thrusts a pointing finger at the people.

"Why were the women and children so quickly drawn into sinful behavior?"

He glares at the assembled crowd, enjoying his moment. He sees his sister staring at him, a frown on her face. *Yes, this includes you,* he thinks, lifting his head higher.

"It is the fault of you husbands and fathers. You have become slack. You're not teaching your wives and children as you should. If you don't discipline them, I will!"

(The Teacher sighs. *Here we go again.*)

The Code Keeper glares out at the miserable crowd.

"Because of this, I am going to apply *the Discipline*, as my father and all Keepers have done in the past."

A soft groan rises from every quarter. The men dutifully, step out to one side of the crowd. They know what is coming and prepare themselves.

The Keeper addresses the rest.

"Those who were in the schoolhouse at the time, are exempt. Return to your studies."

With pitying looks at their other family members, the boys hurry off.

"Women and children are to go home. The men will return later and mete out punishment to *you*. I have no doubt they will administer whatever punishment they see fit!"

Children, who are old enough to understand his words, begin to cry.

The Stalwarts herd the women and young ones back to their homes. When the Stalwarts return, they join with the Healer and Keeper in administering the men's punishment.

Finally, it is over.

The men trudge back to their workstations, carrying their shirts in their hands. Some have old scars reopened, while others have new.

None of the men have any intention of following through on the Keeper's order concerning their families. How can they discipline their wives and children, while they are keeping secrets? There are things concerning the Event at the Tree, which they have not divulged to the Keeper; things they have not spoken about, not even to each other.

When they arrive home at the end of the day, the men quietly inform their families that there will be no discipline, for reasons which they cannot reveal at the moment. However, they need to do *something*. A *token* punishment is agreed on, meted out, and life goes on as before.

The Code Keeper returns to his office, massaging his hands and flexing his aching shoulder. He had no idea that administering the Discipline was such hard and exhausting work. His father had made it look relatively easy. But then, his father had been applying discipline for years.

As far as his *performance* goes, he's very pleased with himself. Everyone listened, and the Discipline was administered without any arguments or resistance on the part of the men. *So this is what it's like being a Code Keeper.* He smiles. *I think I'm going to be okay.*

His thoughts turn to the Great Discipline at the Tree. He has never attended one of *those* disciplines himself. It will be a real test of his caliber as a Code Keeper if the occasion should arise.

He finds himself thinking about the Founder.

How did *he* cope, with the heavy duty of giving discipline? It must have been hard, even for *him,* in the early stages of his leadership.

Chapter 21

What's in a Name?

Pope's mind hadn't stopped working since they arrived at the plateau. New rules, laws, and protocols were constantly presenting themselves.

After assembling the people one morning, Pope made an important announcement.

First, the names they were given at birth, were to be discarded. Names were a part of their former life, a life that no longer existed. To use birth names was now forbidden.

The people were genuinely shocked.

So what was Pope going to call himself?

He proudly announced that he was to be known as 'Code Keeper.' A name which reflected who he was.

The role and title would pass on to his son (when he had one) and to his son's son, and on through the generations to come.

Men would be called by the trade or skill *appointed* to them. For example Blacksmith, Carpenter, Hunter, Leatherman, Weaver and such. The title and role they were given, would remain with them and their generations through all time.

Women would simply be *Woodsman's wife* and so on and so forth. Young ones would be known as *Woodsman's daughter,* or *Woodsman's son,* etcetera.

The people were stunned. How on earth were they going to obey this new rule? As adults, they were going to have a difficult time adjusting. They could only imagine the difficulties the young ones were going to have. What was their

Code Keeper going to do when the children forgot? Beat their names out of them?

(If only they could have seen the future.)

From here and there, angry voices rose up in protest. They'd put up with every other demand, but this was too much.

Pope responded with a furious tirade, reminding them that *he* was the mouthpiece of the Divine. *They* were simply there to obey!

Pope then went on to announce that there would be no holidays, merry-making, celebrations or festivities of *any* kind. The foolish notions and emotions of their old life were done away with, forever.

As Pope was speaking, his eyes fell upon a little girl holding a brightly dressed doll. The sight reminded him of a task he had for the Stalwarts.

The two heavy-handed individuals were ordered to search through the assortment of goods the people had brought with them. Anything that appealed to the "lust of the eyes" or represented "worldly pleasure," was to be taken and placed in a pile before him. Especially anything of bright color.

The Stalwarts were very thorough. They undid bundles, emptied bags, and tossed clothing and bedding all over the place. They were not going to miss a thing.

One poor soul had managed to keep a valuable old violin hidden in his belongings. He had played it a few times in the early stages of their journey but had then become so dispirited that he had put it away. When he saw the Stalwarts manhandling the beautiful old instrument the man felt sick. When they carelessly tossed it onto the pile, he openly wept.

Keeping a watchful eye on the people, Pope took a flaming torch from one of the Stalwarts and set fire to what had become a sizeable bonfire.

All eyes watched the flames consuming clothing, knick-knacks, storybooks, dolls, toys and treasured objects. The people's faces registered a variety of emotions in the fire's flickering light.

Not content with robbing them of their names, their leader was now destroying whatever small pleasures they had left. *What sort of monster was he?*

If ever there was a moment for a mutiny *that* was it. However, the moment passed, with little more than a few whimpers and tears from children.

Turning a deaf ear and a blind eye, Pope announced that they had made a good start. The *Burning* had been inspiring.

Inspiring was not the word his followers would have chosen. The words that some of them were thinking would have *inspired* a thorough flogging if Pope could have read their minds.

After being dismissed, Pope's dejected followers went off to set up temporary shelters. *What horrors was the man going to put them through in the years ahead?*

As Pope lay in his blankets that night, a short distance away from the rest, his eyes caught sight of an enormous tree silhouetted by moonlight, high up on the slope of the escarpment. Something about the tree fascinated him, drew his attention.

As he stared at it, Pope sensed with deep certainty that the tree was going to play a significant role in the years to come.

CHAPTER 22

Winter's moods

Snow swirls over the peaks and rocky crags, blanketing them in white. Branches dip, heavily laden with snow. Icicles hang in glittering arrays from eaves and ledges.

A deer wanders out from the snow-laden trees, its hooves sinking into the soft snow. Its breath comes in white puffs, and there is a dusting of white on its coat.

Upon the high ridgeline, there is an extraordinary sight. Snow flurries and ice crystals are giving swirling chase to a figure in a cloak of glittering white; a figure who dashes and darts along the peaks and rocky crags, teasing the flurries and sending snow, swirling in all directions. The snowflakes drift back down, gently laughing, covering his cheeks in soft, cold kisses.

He has not forgotten the people of the Code. Even while he dances and celebrates the beauty of the season, his music is doing its work.

Autumn's beautiful prelude over, it bows gracefully and leaves the stage. Winter makes its grand entrance, playing its Ballade in cold flurries and icy blasts.

Snow falls, banking up until at times it's hard to tell where a snow-bank ends and a house begins.

As usual, winter brings strange moods and tales.

Many whisper about hearing singing in the swirling snow flurries. Some tell of seeing a shadow passing, however, they never actually see anyone.

Sometimes, individuals report seeing the cloaked stranger, just for a moment in their peripheral vision, but when they turn to look, there is nobody there.

Children tell of a person singing to them after they've woken up crying from a nightmare. If it isn't their mother, who is it?

Fleeting glimpses of shadows, cloaked strangers, singing, music in the winds; all of these tales find their way to the ears of the Code Keeper who, with the sagely wisdom inherited from his father, dismisses it all as "delusional imaginings of inferior minds."

Generally speaking, the Code Keeper is satisfied with how he is running things. Despite the foolish notions and stories, the people are going about their tasks as they should. The Discipline apparently worked.

Things may have appeared *normal* to the Code Keeper, however, for the men who had made the trek to the Tree, life is anything *but* normal.

The stories they hear of singing, music, and glimpses of a man in a cloak, are adding to their nightmares. Night after night they wake up sweating, reliving the event at the Tree, every detail etched in their minds. They look forward to their work hours. At least they can get some momentary respite by concentrating on their tasks.

As for the Healer, who lives in a world of steaming lotions and potions, he is unaware of anything except his satisfaction at performing his duties well.

The Teacher's wife gave birth to a girl, and other births have been trouble-free. The people are in good health. Those who reached the appointed Age, have been *moved on*. The balance is being kept.

The Healer often thinks about the Law of Age.

Not wanting limited resources wasted on the old or infirm, the Founder introduced the Law of Age, which demands that as soon as an individual reaches an appointed age, they are to *pass on*. The Healer *assists* by administering a tisane which will enable a pain-free, dignified exit from the world. The people are not given a choice about it. It's practical and for the good of the community as a whole.

(That's what they've been taught anyway. The Healer has to confess that sometimes, he wonders...?)

Winter quits the stage and spring dances on. Summer waits in the wings, keen to make her entrance.

The Teacher's mind has become a battlefield. According to the Founder, Divine Judgment fell and destroyed *all* sinners in the world below, beginning with the Founder's town.

"If that is the case," ponders the Teacher, "where do the random strangers come from?"

One day, as the irritating question circles his head for the millionth time, a name leaps into his thoughts—*the Traveler!* If anyone knew the truth of things in the world below, he would!

For a moment, hope flares up, then it quickly fades. Travelers are not permitted to speak with other villagers.

The Teacher sighs loudly in his frustration. Is he ever going to get any answers? *Will it matter if he does? It certainly won't change anything.*

Spring has had her turn on the stage, and summer is fluffing her skirts. She is ready to dance into the spotlight.

The Traveler's wife looks out from the door of their log cabin, at the farthest end of the plateau. Her husband and son are loading skins and furs onto the pack-horses. (The Hunters leave them in bundles, at a spot near the end of the trail.)

Her husband is about to head down through the mountains. Every year, he heads off to the lowlands and is gone for many weeks, returning just before the next heavy winter snows set in. He brings back items which the Code Keepers store away under lock and key until required.

The Traveler's wife laughs to herself.

It was one of their predecessors who lugged the iron water pump back. *What a cumbersome piece that would have been!*

She gazes at their beautiful surroundings. What more could they ask for? They live a simple, peaceful life. She is glad they live apart from the main village. Their lives are free from the constant monitoring and intrusion of Code Keepers, Healers, and Stalwarts. Nobody comes near them unless sent by the Code Keeper for a particular purpose. Even then, there is no *conversation*.

The Founder decreed that Travelers be isolated so they would not be tempted to communicate about what is seen or heard in the lands below. They are not permitted to divulge information to anyone, not even their family or Code Keepers.

The Traveler's wife gives a small "hmph" and focuses on more pleasant things. Their son! He is a great help to his father and is doing well in the village school. He enjoys the run through the fields to the schoolhouse in the mornings and is always glad to leave the village at the end of the day.

The horses are loaded up, and everything is ready. The Traveler comes over for a final embrace, hugs his son, and heads out. In a moment, he and the horses are swallowed by the trees.

His wife prays he will have a safe journey and a speedy return.

The Traveler works his way down through the forest, breathing in the rich air and enjoying his surroundings. He loves their lifestyle; loves the freedom of it. He also enjoys the fact that he can leave the plateau. He wishes his family could go with him. Maybe one day things will change. He hopes so.

The Traveler finds it staggering that after so many generations, the people are still ignorant of anything beyond their community. He'd have thought that at some point, *someone* would have ventured down from the plateau. Those who are exiled may perhaps, find their way through the wilderness of mountains and forests, but he doubts it. There are wolves, bears, and mountain lions, always looking for easy prey.

The Traveler shakes his head and sighs deeply. The leaders are coldly calculating in their decisions.

The most difficult thing for Travelers is the silence they must maintain about all that they see and hear in their travels. No Traveler has ever broken that silence. They care for their family's safety and well-being too much.

Like his father before him, the Traveler hopes and prays that *someone* will come and break the terrible chains binding the people; or that someone else will pluck up the courage to head out on their own.

His thoughts turn to the people he meets in the lowlands. They believe he is a loner who wanders the country, bartering for personal reasons. He doesn't correct them.

Over time, *Lowlanders* have become accustomed to the *silent men* from the mountains, who come and go without fuss or bother. If any Lowlander took it into their head to follow a Traveler back, there is an entire system of confusing cut-backs and challenging paths through the mountain wilderness; tracks and routes cleverly planned and disguised by his forebears. Any would-be followers would become lost.

"*They could never be as lost as the people of the Code,*" he thinks with a mournful shake of his head.

Chapter 23

Shadows in the Snow

The summer season is in full swing; wildflowers are abundant, and the droning of insects fills the air. Nature is enjoying herself and showing off.

Summer turns into autumn beautiful and alluring in the reds and golds of her skirts and petticoats.

Not wanting to wait in the wings any longer, winter runs onto the stage in full costume and frenzied dance, catching everyone by surprise. The weary Traveler in particular.

He is struggling homeward, but the soft snow is deep. It reaches above the horses' girths. Soon they are making no headway at all; just floundering and getting nowhere.

Snow and temperatures continue to plummet.

The Traveler's dry rations are gone, and he discovers, that at some point, his flint has fallen from his belt. No fire means no chance of survival.

Wolves have been tracking them and judging by their howls they are not far off.

The Traveler figures he may as well make a stand. However, the only weapon he has is his hunting knife. On its own, it isn't going to be much use against an entire pack of hungry wolves.

The Traveler regards his three horses with a heavy heart. *The poor beasts will have to fend for themselves.*

He digs in against the rough trunk of a tree and waits. The horses huddle together, hemmed in by the thick snow.

He wonders how his wife and son will cope without him. The boy is not yet ready to take on the role of Traveler. What will the leaders do?

The exhausted Traveler tries to keep his eyes open but slowly sinks into what feels like soft, embracing feathers.

Snow continues falling. The cold is intense.

The forest echoes with loud snaps and cracks.

Ghostly shapes materialize out of the grayness, their cautious approach muffled by the snow. Slowly they creep closer.

A flurry of snow sweeps through the pack. A tall figure materializes and approaches the Traveler, who is sleeping deeply...too deeply. It is the sleep which befalls those caught and held fast in winter's cold, icy grip.

The man bends down close and breathes on the still and silent Traveler.

"Not yet, dear friend. You still have much to do."

The figure then moves a short distance away.

Standing in the falling snow, the man begins to sing.

The wolves instantly start leaping and bounding about like playful puppies, ingratiating themselves to him, for they know he is *the Alpha*. Cries and yelps fill the air.

The Traveler is oblivious to the jubilant scene taking place.

As the man sings, a large patch of green appears. Paying no mind to the frolicking wolves, the horses shuffle forward and begin grazing on the exposed new grass. The wolves pay no heed to them.

Gathering some branches, the man tosses them into a pile, which immediately bursts into flame. Settling himself beside the warm, crackling fire, he watches over the sleeping Traveler, while continuing to sing.

Chapter 24

Desperate for a Miracle

Spring has arrived, announcing her presence with dripping icicles and warm sighs. Flowers stretch and yawn as they push themselves up through thinning, melting snow.

The Code Keeper is bursting with fresh zeal and enthusiasm. He strides from building to building, to watch the men at work. Before long he is critiquing their efforts; pointing out what they are doing wrong and following this with *his* idea of how things *should* be done. He also takes it into his head to dole out on the spot discipline. No need to follow *formal* protocols. He may as well deal with any problem on the spot!

Exasperated beyond measure, the men wish he would leave them alone. They've been doing these tasks for generation after generation. Their skills have been refined and honed. What skill does the Code Keeper have? He is, to put it bluntly, *just* a Code Keeper. He and his miserable predecessors have exercised no skills other than barking orders, giving dull sermons and doling out discipline with that 'stinking' horsewhip, *Righteousness!*

All in all, their new Code Keeper is proving worse than his father. At least, his father followed protocol, and they knew how things were and where they stood. This young upstart is as unpredictable as a hornet and has a temper to match.

Some of the villagers look longingly toward the forest bordering the plateau, their heads filled with dreams of escape. Their dreaming is short-lived, however. All of them know they are ill-equipped to deal with whatever is below the plateau, let alone below the mountains.

So, while Arrogance and Zeal sing their loud, raucous melodies through the over-zealous young Code Keeper; Anger, Resentment, and Despair sing gloomy songs in the people's hearts.

The *Other* is feeling placated. It may have taken a beating a while back. However, it has been weaving its oppressive music and is seeing results. The music of its enemy is being dampened and suppressed in many hearts.

The *Other* grins. All it has to do is be patient, in the manner of a lion waiting for prey. It isn't that difficult. Anger, resentment, despair, bitterness, un-forgiveness all of these things weaken the soul, rendering it vulnerable to attack.

Humanity doesn't understand that its hatred is not for the fact that they *exist*, it's more for the fact that *He* created them, loves them and wants good things for them. *That's* what it hates most. Plus the fact that miserable humanity is being given the choice of accepting an eternal future, which *it* has lost forever!

So, it will continue weaving its destructive melodies to make souls question and doubt the songs of the enemy. It's greatest success, is when offering an alluring *alternative* melody.

It used *this* little trick eons ago, with the most profound and satisfying results; in a garden if it remembers correctly.

Time has passed, and the Healer is getting concerned. The people are going about their tasks in a sullen robotic fashion, and it worries him. He also has a frightening suspicion that their numbers are in decline.

The Healer is reluctant to relay his thoughts to the Code Keeper, for the Keeper would hold *him* personally responsible. After all, it's the job of Healers to monitor and control these things. The lives of the people are, in a manner of speaking, in his hands. *Well, most of the time.*

The Healer shudders as he thinks of the Elder who, for some strange reason or another, headed off into the forest below the plateau, during peak winter snows.

When the Elder's family reported him missing, the Stalwarts went searching. All they found was a trail of discarded clothing. Of the Elder, there was no sign.

The leaders concluded that the Elder had gone into the forest naked, and perished from the cold. They also advised that it was useless looking for him because he'd either be buried under snow or animals would have gotten to him.

The question, of course, was *why* did the Elder do it?

The Code Keeper believes that the man's mind had slipped. He made this announcement to the people and ordered no further gossip or discussion on the matter.

The Healer thinks that the Keeper's order is ludicrous. Speculation would be rife in every home.

The Healer is right.

Those who had known the Elder personally, believe (among themselves), that it was the Elder's way of thumbing his nose at the Law of Age! The Elder had often said to them, "No Healer is going to shove poison down *my* throat."

They wisely keep their thoughts to themselves. As it is, they aren't sure whether to cheer the Elder or call him an idiot.

The Healer finds himself affected by the Elder's actions. He cannot understand them. It seems a foolish thing to do when *he* could have given the Elder a dignified, pain-free *release*. He hopes that others, who are approaching the Age, will not be tempted to copy the man.

Prayer is not something the Healer is given to. However, he finds himself muttering a few prayers now and again, in the hope that things will start to turn around. He'd like something positive to happen, a miracle perhaps? Something that will bring life into the community, before the Code Keeper starts noticing and asking him questions!

As it turns out, a *miracle* has already occurred. Although not the kind the Healer is hoping for.

When the Traveler finally clumped in through their cabin door, covered in snow, his hair and beard frosted white, his wife and son were ecstatic. They'd been gravely concerned about his lateness and had worried that something untoward might have happened.

The story he told, left his family bug-eyed.

He said that he must have fallen into a deep sleep because he'd woken up all a sudden, to find a clearing of green grass, his horses grazing, and a stranger sitting by a fire. The stranger had been singing, and wolves had been sleeping all around him. The stranger showed him a path (which hadn't been there before) and told him to follow it, for it would lead him home. The man had also assured him that he would arrive back with no loss of horse, baggage or harm to himself.

Thankful, and not wanting to delay any longer, the Traveler and his horses, set out on the path. He'd turned for one last look at the stranger and seen the man disappearing into the forest, with wolves cavorting around him like puppies. He'd heard the man's singing for a while; then everything had fallen silent.

The Traveler had followed the path, as directed, and here he was! Home, safe and sound!

His family agreed that a miracle had taken place. As for the stranger, they wondered who it could have been.

It's a pity none of the villagers could have heard the Traveler's story. It would have given them hope that somewhere, out there, *someone* existed who knew of their oppressed lives and would come to help.

They were people in desperate need of a miracle.

Chapter 25

A New Arrival

He is deeply aware of the suffering in the village, for he hears every painful refrain in their hearts.

Yes, the Other has been busy and thinks it has succeeded in crushing his music. However, (he smiles) being a deceiver by nature, the Other always ends up deceiving itself even more.

As for his own songs: they brought all things into being, and breathe life. They always will, for the mere fact of Who he is and was, and always will be.

Some call him 'Singer.' It is a name which describes what he does, along with other names that declare his character and his nature. He does have a name by which many know him, and it is a name of Power and Authority. A Name, which is above every other name.

Those who live in companionship with him, share his songs and have his music in their hearts. They live under his banner, and he gives them his Name.

The people of the Code will soon learn these things for themselves. In the meantime...

It is an idyllic sunny morning. Boys are in school; women are busy in their homes. Tailors are mending, Carpenters are engaged in carpentry, and Hunters are hunting, and so on and so forth.

The Pickers are patrolling the village surrounds, as usual, looking for flowers bearing the bright colors of sin. One of them spots movement at the edge of the forest. They go to investigate.

When they reach the forest edge, they are stunned to see a small boy sitting on a tree stump. He is playing with a pinecone, idly tossing it from one hand to the other. It's not one of the village boys, so who is he and where has he come from?

The two men pepper him with questions.

"Who are you?"

"Where are your parents?"

"Is anyone with you?"

The boy remains silent through the interrogation.

The two men explore the immediate area, calling out, in case an adult is in the vicinity. However, there is no response from any quarter. The boy must have strayed from somewhere and gotten himself lost on a grand scale. It's amazing that he has survived the wilds, not to mention wolves, bears and mountain lions.

They decide to take him back to the Great House. The Keeper will know what to do.

The boy seems happy to accompany them.

In the Great House, the Keeper spends some moments trying to communicate with the boy. However, no responses are forthcoming. The Keeper comes to the conclusion that the boy is unable to speak due to some physical condition. Despite this, the boy appears healthy, albeit dirty, scruffy and overly scrawny, due to his time in the wilds.

The Keeper ponders what to do with the child. Perhaps he can be adopted by the Traveler? They are sworn to silence, so what better than a future Traveler who cannot speak?

He orders the Stalwarts to take the child to the Traveler's home.

The family is delighted when the young lad is delivered to their door. The boy can go to school with their son, who will be glad to have a companion. The other boys tend to shun him. (They are jealous of the fact that he gets to wander through the fields of the plateau, on his way to and from school.)

As the weeks pass, the boy proves he has a quick and intelligent mind. His enthusiasm for his lessons encourages the younger ones to do well and challenges the older students to do better. None of them wants to be outdone by a "dummy" (as they unkindly call him).

The Teacher wonders where the boy hails from, however, seeing as the child is unable to speak, it is pointless asking him.

The Traveler and his family are enjoying the young boy's presence. Especially their son.

After school, the two boys run and romp freely in the fields around the log cabin, chasing rabbits, leaping over logs and stumps in their hot pursuit. There is no chance they will catch any. The Traveler's son makes enough noise for the two of them; shouting and yelling the whole time.

The boy appears perfectly happy with them, and they treat him as their own, so all is working out well.

One morning, the Traveler rounds the corner of the cabin to find the young boy kneeling in the meadow-grass a short distance away. A Falcon is sitting on the boy's shoulder and around him are half a dozen rabbits. The Traveler steps back so he can observe without being noticed.

It appears as if the little group is simply enjoying each other's company.

The Traveler's son comes charging out of the cabin, calling for the boy. In a flash, the rabbits are gone, and the Falcon ascends into the sky.

There are other occasions when the Traveler sees a similar interaction between the boy and nature. However, he keeps the knowledge of these things to himself, sensing that the boy's quiet interactions with nature are something personal and precious.

It is not just the boy who has special moments.

The Traveler's son wakes up very early one morning and notices his father is not in the cabin. He waits for a while. However, his father still doesn't appear. Quietly, so he won't disturb the others, the Traveler's son tiptoes outside to see where his father is.

As he walks around the cabin, the Traveler's son thinks he can hear talking, so he follows the sound and comes across his father. He is standing in the forest, apparently having a conversation with someone.

The Traveler's son tries to see who his father is speaking with. However, he can't see anyone. It's all a bit strange. Not wanting to disturb his father, he quietly returns to the cabin.

One evening, while they are all sitting around the fire, the boy plucks up the courage to ask his father about his conversation in the woods.

The Traveler smiles and explains that he is talking to the person who created everything.

"How do you know someone made everything?"

The Traveler ruffles his son's hair.

"Just look at the skies at night. Is all of that splendor just a mistake? A freak accident of nature?"

The Traveler smiles warmly.

"Look at Nature around you. Look at the intricate shapes and patterns; see how things are formed. Careful design went into it all. Everything is a part of a Whole. From the smallest to the greatest, they contribute to the vast cycle of life. I have deep respect for creation, and so should you."

His son thinks for a moment.

"What about when we kill things?"

The Traveler leans forward.

"We hunt for food, and we use what we need for practical reasons. However, we do not misuse or abuse. Do you understand what I am saying?"

His son nods.

The other lad is listening intently.

"So how do you know this person hears you?"

Patting his son's head, the Traveler laughs.

"Well, it's common sense, isn't it? Remember when you spent days building your cart? How did you feel when you had finished it? Were you happy with it? Did you love it?"

His son nods enthusiastically.

"Well then, imagine being the one who made all of this, (he spreads his arms wide) including people. Do you think *he's* pleased with what he made? Do you think he looks at it and says, "This is really good?" I believe he does. Whoever created the world and the wonders within it, is somebody worth knowing, don't you think? Someone worth talking to?"

The Traveler laughs.

"I may be the one doing most of the talking, but I have a feeling that he listens and enjoys our *conversations*."

As the boy thinks about all that his father has said, his face lights up.

"Father, remember the miracle in the snow? The mysterious person who helped you?"

His father nods. *What's the boy going to come out with now?*
"Maybe he was the person you talk to! You said the wolves liked him, and you said the horses were happy too."

The Traveler is astounded. *By the Code, the lad could be right!*

The Traveler excuses himself and hurries outside. He's got some heartfelt thanks he wants to pass on.

That night, after the two boys are settled in their beds, the Traveler's son whispers to his young friend, that *he* is going to start talking to the person who made everything. He's got a lot of questions to ask him.

His young friend, who is lying with his back to the Traveler's son, grins broadly.

While life in the Traveler's home continues on its happy way, those living within the confines of the village, are being driven crazy.

Their over-zealous Code Keeper is now likening himself to an ancient prophet called *Moses*, who led an entire race of people out of slavery, setting them free from the tyrannical rule of someone called *Pharaoh*.

"Foolish nonsense," one of the Elders keeps muttering to the others. "When is this green sapling going to grow up!"

The people have their own interpretation of the *Moses* story.

Their over-zealous Code Keeper is *Pharaoh*, and *they* are the slaves! Now all they need is a *Moses* to come and deliver *them!*

Sadly, the chances of that happening are zero to none. The only person to make an appearance in recent times, was the stranger, a vagrant in a long cloak, and all *he* did was sing! What good was that?

Chapter 26

Butterflies and Mayhem

The stranger is standing in the shadows of the forest trees. Above him, on a large branch, sits the eagle.

The stranger looks up at the great bird.

"*So, what do you think of our little community?*"

The eagle turns its head in the direction of the village and lets out a series of squawks.

"*What do you mean, "They're all a bunch of chickens?""*

The eagle screeches, stretches out its wings, and does a side-step dance on the branch.

"*Dear friend, you know you are an eagle, and your young ones know they are eagles. These poor people don't know what they are.*"

The eagle turns a bright yellow eye on the stranger and chitters in its throat.

"*You don't have a very high opinion of them, do you? What's wrong with chickens anyway?*"

The eagle bobs its head and emits a series of cries and squawks.

"*Oh, I see. Chickens are an inferior species, and eagles eat chickens! For your information, I am going to turn these chickens into eagles. What do you think of that?*"

The eagle indulges in the nearest thing to a snort that an eagle can do, screeches and launches itself into the air in a huff.

The eagle's companion sighs.

"*You have no sense of humor, do you know that?*"

～ৎ～

The Teacher hands out the lessons for the day and returns to his desk, where he sits gazing out the schoolroom window. His thoughts swim leisurely through the green and gold fields around them. Bees can be heard droning around the hives not too far away. Not a breath of wind stirs.

A butterfly dances in through the open window.

At first, the Teacher doesn't register it, but when he does, he sits up quickly. Looking left and right, he tries to pinpoint where the creature is. Finally, he spots it and gasps! It is resting on the up-stretched fingers of the new boy, who is studying the butterfly, with a huge smile on his face.

The other students are watching, intrigued.

The Teacher is aghast. Something so small can bring trouble down on their heads if not dealt with immediately.

He carefully approaches the boy. Before he has gone two steps, however, a second butterfly waltzes its way into the schoolroom. It dances around the children before settling on the young boy's hand, as the first had done.

The Teacher picks up a book, intending to swat the creatures. To his amazement, however, dozens more float into the room, elegantly fluttering their way to the boy, who now looks as if he is wearing a living, multi-colored cloak.

The other students are in awe.

One of them stretches out his hand, hoping to touch the lovely creatures. As he does, the event which triggers everything else occurs.

The young boy *speaks*.

The blood drains from the Teacher's face.

As the lovely melody flows from the boy's lips, more butterflies drift in through the open window, joining the others in their fluttering dance around the boy.

The Teacher is having difficulty breathing. Panic is rising; he exits the building. In his haste, he stumbles and falls sprawling in the street.

The Code Keeper, who is standing on the steps of the Great House, sees the Teacher fall. He strides toward the Teacher and hears the sounds coming from the schoolroom. Without stopping to check on the Teacher, he bursts into the building, halting at the sight that greets him. There is the boy, almost invisible in a cloud of butterflies, and to the Keeper's horror, the boy is singing.

The stressed Teacher re-enters the schoolroom. Neither of the men knows what to do.

The boy decides for them, by walking out of the schoolroom and into the street, with many of the butterflies still clinging to him, while others flutter around him in a bright, colorful cloud.

The younger students decide to run outside and join him. They're thrilled with what is happening. They never have adventures, and this is a great one. The very best!

The Teacher's son, however, is too frightened to join them. When he sees that everyone's attention is elsewhere, he runs home, keeping to the rear of the buildings so that he won't be seen.

Other children who have heard the noises, run out of their homes and join the merry procession. There is now a colorful parade, with butterflies, singing, and laughing children.

The Keeper snaps out of his shock and sprints back to the Great House, shouting for the Stalwarts to bring their horsewhips.

The Teacher now has a dilemma. Should he stay in the schoolroom with the rest of the students or should he try to get the children back inside, before the fury of the leaders descends upon them? He opts for the second and heads out of the schoolroom. Unfortunately, he is too late.

The Keeper and Stalwarts are already among the children, scattering them with calculated blows of their horsewhips, driving them away from the boy and the butterflies.

Children run to their homes, crying from the stinging blows and terrified of the three angry men.

The Teacher can do nothing now. He watches from nearby, his anger rising.

With rough hands, the Keeper and Stalwarts, grab and snatch at the delicate creatures with no thought for the damage they are doing to the fragile wings or small bodies.

The boy has stopped his singing and is standing very still. His eyes are fixed on the angry leaders and there is a strange expression on his face.

Exhausted from their efforts and seeing they have succeeded in getting rid of the offending creatures, the three men now turn their attention to the boy himself.

"Take him to my office," the Keeper snaps.

Those who have observed the amazing scene, are too stunned to say or do anything. It has all happened so quickly. They wander off with heavy hearts, wishing they'd had the courage to step in.

The Teacher is left standing alone. Scattered around him are crushed butterflies, their wings torn and broken. He can hear children crying in the houses nearby. He has no trouble imagining the welts and bruises inflicted by the angry men.

Kneeling down, he picks up one of the broken butterflies. The lovely little creature struggles feebly.

"If there *is* a God, I hope you see this!" he whispers hoarsely.

His face burning and emotions roiling, he strides back to the schoolroom, where he brusquely orders the remaining students to go to their homes, and stay there. At that moment he couldn't care less about classes or routines. If the Code Keeper decides to take the horsewhip to him, he'll probably rip the dratted thing out of the Keeper's hands and throw it to the pigs, the Keeper right behind!

The Teacher is fully primed and ready to launch a full-scale revolution.

As he heads toward his house, he mutters angrily about the things he'd like to do to the Code Keeper and those two brutes called *Stalwarts*.

On entering his home, the Teacher slams the door so hard behind him that it rebounds, clouting him in the head. Infuriated, he slams the door again, receiving another hard knock as a result.

"Damned cursed door," he shouts.

He wonders if anyone outside has noticed his temper tantrum. "Too bad," he snaps angrily.

When his wife hears the racket and accompanying expletives, she braces herself.

The Teacher rages into the kitchen, shaking both his fists in the air and growling through his teeth like an angry bear.

His wife tenses.

The Teacher sees it and is quick to reassure her.

"It's not you! Please, it's not you!"

He has the grace to look ashamed, remembering his behavior and harsh words to her some time back. Quickly, he tells her about the butterflies and what has happened. The Teacher decides there is no point in holding anything back. She might as well hear *everything*.

As she listens to his account of what happened at the Tree, her face pales, and her heart beats fast. *What on earth is going on?*

"Do you know why you are here, in the Great House?"

The Keeper is questioning the boy. However, the child is paying no attention. Instead, he makes shapes with his fingers while quietly humming to himself.

"Stop that noise at once!" the Keeper orders sharply.

The boy drops his hands and stares at the Keeper, his young face expressionless.

The Keeper and Healer move to the far end of the room, to discuss the situation. It is clear to both of them that bringing the boy into the village was a bad mistake. Who is responsible?

The Pickers! It's *their* fault. They should have cast the boy back into the forest and left him there. *They* will be disciplined!

The decision is made to remove the boy before other unacceptable events occur. They have the Stalwarts put the lad in the room at the rear of the Great House.

The two men are then sent off, to advise the Traveler that they will no longer be required to look after him.

The news saddens the Travelers wife. They will miss him terribly.

The Traveler says nothing when the Stalwarts give them the news. He merely nods. The leaders think he is ignorant of what goes on in the village. However, he *knows* what happens to strangers and those who are unwanted. *He knows many things.*

Back in the Teacher's home, all is quiet.

The Teacher is sitting with his elbows on the table, his head in his hands. The tale has been told. He has shared it all and left nothing out. Lifting his head, he stares at her.

"This incident with the boy is the last straw. We *have* to do something!"

He gets up and pulls on his jacket, which he had tossed aside on his arrival. Running his fingers through his hair, he sighs deeply.

His wife touches his face gently.

"There is something I need to share with you before you go. It won't take a moment."

The Teacher's face turns gray when he hears about the music the women listen to, and the battle on the path.

"I *knew* it! Strange things are happening, and I'm sure the stranger has something to do with it all. The boy may be a part of it as well."

The Teacher's voice snags for a second.

"What are we dealing with here?"

His face is full of pain.

"We have to stop our leaders from doing further harm."

He finishes fastening his coat and turns toward the door.

"If I can get the other men to come with me, there is a chance."

He reaches for the door, then turns and pulls her into his arms. Burying his face in her hair, he whispers, "I'm sorry...for everything. I have not been kind to you." Then he is gone.

His wife stands unmoving, a blush of pink on her cheeks and hand over her heart, which is beating oddly for some strange reason.

CHAPTER 27

A Full-scale Mutiny

The Stalwart almost jumps out of his skin! Someone is pounding on the door of the Great House as if determined to knock it down. He opens it and is staggered to see the village men, including the Elders, standing in a crowd outside.

"What do you want?" he growls, glaring at them.

The Teacher is in no mood for a bullying Stalwart.

"Stand aside! We have business with the Code Keeper."

The Stalwart is about to protest when he notices the expressions on the men's faces and the horsewhips in their hands. It dawns on him that if they deal with him as he has often dealt with them, he will not escape injury. The Stalwart steps aside.

The Keeper is still in his office discussing the day's events with the Healer. He cannot believe his eyes when the door opens, and the men pour in, cramming the room and hallway.

"What are you doing in this building?" he bellows, snatching up *Righteousness*.

"Where is the boy?" demands the Teacher.

"Are you insane?" the Keeper thunders. "Do you know what this intrusion is going to cost you?"

The Teacher stands his ground.

To keep the wily leaders in check, he asks some of the men to bind the Keeper and Healer to their chairs. Both men shout threats and warnings. Their shouts are ignored.

Hearing the ruckus, the two Stalwarts barge into the room, prepared to do battle. However, they are no match for the determined men.

The Teacher asks somebody to go to the back room, but they return, advising that the cell is empty. A search reveals no sign of the boy anywhere. Perhaps he's gone home to the Traveler and his family?

The Teacher has a feeling that wherever the boy is, he's alright.

The Keeper glares around the room, his face dark with rage.

"You will pay dearly for this," he thunders.

The Teacher leans over.

"There will be no "paying dearly." We've had enough! This wretched reign of Code Keepers, Healers and Stalwarts is over! Finished!"

The Keeper's mouth falls open.

"Finished? Over? What are you talking about?"

The Teacher makes it abundantly clear that the Founder's cruel laws and protocols are no longer going to be tolerated.

The Keeper is stunned. *This is outright rebellion. It's a mutiny! It's...*

The Teacher sees that the young man is about to arc up. Not wanting to waste time on heated arguments, he decides it's time to reveal what happened at the Tree. It might make the Keeper listen to everything else they have to say. *One can only hope.*

"You once asked if there was anything to add concerning the stranger. Well, there is plenty to add, and you are now going to hear it."

The Code Keeper opens his mouth to make some remark. However, the Teacher isn't having any of it. He orders that the four leaders be gagged. Temporarily of course! It's the only way to ensure he gets no interruptions.

Taking a deep breath and with murmurs of encouragement from the surrounding men, the Teacher begins his account.

"All of us headed out along the path, the stranger walking between the Stalwarts. He appeared calm and sometimes we could hear him humming under his breath. We thought it bizarre, considering the situation.

We entered the shadows of the trees and climbed the trail to the grassy plateau where the Great Tree stands. If you have not seen it, all I can tell you is that it was a gigantic tree that was twisted and bent, as if it had suffered in some terrible way, or contracted a sickness.

When we got to the Tree, the Code Keeper placed his hands upon its trunk and looking upwards, prayed the traditional prayer.

"We have come to honor the Code. Evil has come into our midst. It has sought to disrupt our ways and threatened the purity of our people. We destroy the evil so that good may continue. Amen."

After this prayer, the Stalwarts tore the cloak from the stranger and flung it away. Then, at the Code Keeper's direction, they bound the stranger to the Tree face first, using ropes which some of us had carried up. The Code Keeper said that fastening someone to the Tree that way, was very symbolic of someone *embracing* their fate!"

(The Keeper's eyebrows shoot upward. *Had his father been given to dark humor? Surely not!*)

"As the Stalwarts checked the ropes binding the stranger, the man began to sing. We ignored it, for his singing was going to end soon enough!"

The Teacher falls silent. In his mind, he is back at the Tree. *That poor, twisted Tree.*

The *poor, twisted Tree* had a story of its own.

As the stranger's singing had filtered down into its heart, the ancient Tree had woken from its slumbers.

So had its memory.

The Tree remembered being a rough-shelled seed, cocooned in the soft earth. Sun had warmed the earth and rain had watered it. The shell had cracked, and a tender shoot had emerged, pushing its way up through the fertile soil, finally breaking free into the warm sunlight.

Over the centuries, the Tree had continued to grow in strength and stature, with wide spreading branches and a large crown of leafy green foliage.

The Tree had loved its life of constantly changing seasons, the nesting of birds in its branches, the soft grass that grew beneath, through which wildflowers pushed their way in spring and summer.

Then a darkness had come.

Men, strange creatures that they were, had visited the Tree. They had admired its mighty stature and strength. Soon after their visit, they had returned. To the Tree's horror, they had fastened one of their own against its trunk, before falling upon the man and violently whipping the life from him.

The Tree had heard the blows and felt the man's pain. The earth below had shuddered as it took in the lifeblood of the human creature.

The Tree had felt something *twist* deep within its core.

As the years passed by, other lives were fastened to the Tree, and as each life had been poured out upon its blood-stained bark, the Tree had become increasingly sick of heart.

No longer did it stand tall and proud. In an agony of shame and sorrow it began to withdraw into itself; finally falling into a deep, merciful, numbing sleep—sleep that continued undisturbed...until the sound of singing pierced through the darkness.

Recognizing the voice and the one who sang, the Tree had sung a heart-rending song of its own...a desperate cry to be released from its pain.

The singer's reply had made the ancient Tree weep with joy, its tears of rich, red sap unnoticed by the angry men gathered around it.

The Teacher draws a deep breath. He had been reliving the moments at the Tree and wondering how they could ever have considered such cruelty *acceptable*.

Shaking his head at the senseless horror of it all, he continues his narration.

"The storm clouds we had seen earlier, were now a dark swirling mass of purple and black, directly above us. Lightning was flashing, and there were great rolls of thunder. Blue light, like fire, began sizzling along the ground. With every crash of thunder, the earth trembled beneath our feet.

We drew back, distancing ourselves from the Tree and the stranger, but your fathers stood firm, refusing to be intimidated by what they called, a "freak show of nature." Your father, the Code Keeper, poised to make the first strike with his whip."

The Teacher's voice breaks, and he swallows.

"The stranger's singing had grown stronger; his song more powerful."

He pauses.

"Don't hold back," murmurs one of the Elders, who is standing close by. "They need to hear it all."

The Teacher nods and takes a deep breath.

"What happened next was beyond belief. We heard strange sounds coming from the cloud above us. All I can liken them to is the sound made on the Animal Keeper's ram's horn. The one he uses to call in the animals. On top of that, we could see flashes of white light darting backward and forwards through the cloud. They were not lightning flashes. We were puzzled as to what they might be. The lights appeared to have a purpose, for they *presented* themselves to the stranger before flashing upwards again."

(The Code Keeper blinks. *Is the Teacher seriously expecting him to believe all this?*)

"There was nothing *natural* about all that was happening. I remember standing there wondering, "*Who is this man?*""

The Teacher's voice fades. There is silence in the room. He looks at the Code Keeper.

"Your father refused to be put off by what was happening. Instead of marveling or showing fear, he was seething with rage. I confess I have never seen such fury in a man, and I could not understand it.

Your father thrust *Righteousness* skyward as if shoving it into the face of the storm, and he began shouting madly that, "no god, trumpets or flashes of light" were going to prevent him from doing what *he* was there to do."

(The eyes of the bound men focus intently on the Teacher.)

"Your fathers then set upon the stranger. I saw their whips fly into motion. *In that instant*, there was a mighty 'CRACK.' A great bolt of lightning speared downward, directly into the heart of the Tree. The blast was incredible."

The Teacher pauses, reliving the terrifying moment.

"We were flung backward, as if by a giant hand. When we got to our feet, we saw that the Tree was gone. Only a blackened, shattered stump remained, smoke rising from its blasted core. The ground all around was scorched black. The lightning bolt had obliterated the Tree from top to bottom. Nothing remained of it, apart from that black smoking crater.

We looked for your fathers and the stranger. However, all we saw were burnt, blackened remains on the outer edge of the clearing. I'm glad you were not there to see the awful sight."

The Teacher looks around the room. The next piece of information is critical. He coughs and clears his throat nervously.

"When we turned our eyes back to the ruined Tree, we could not believe what we saw. Standing beside the smoldering stump, *completely unharmed*, was the stranger.

I think I'd be right in saying that *all* of us began to consider the possibility that the person standing in front of us was a Divine Agent, or the Divine himself."

(*Divine Agent? The Divine?* Is the Teacher serious? The Code Keeper rolls his eyes and shakes his head.)

The Teacher continues as if he hasn't seen the Keeper's reaction.

"With that thought in our minds, we waited for him to strike us down or exact vengeance on us in some way. However, he did nothing. I can honestly say that there was no hint of animosity on his face or anger in his stance."

The Tailor chose to interrupt at this point.

"Tell them about the stranger's cloak. Describe the cloak."

The Teacher nodded, but before he could speak, one of the Weavers butted in, his words pouring out in a breathless rush.

"I have never seen a garment like it. The colors were beautiful, astounding. It was as if all the colors of nature were in its warp and weft. Colors that were in constant motion, rippling and shifting. Why, even the storm above us seemed to be woven into its folds, for we could see the storm's colors and flashes of lightning dancing and flickering. I swear I could hear thunder rumbling within the fabric..."

The Weaver stops for breath. *What's come over him? He's never been so 'gabby.'*

The Teacher clears his throat, and with a smile at the red-faced Weaver, he takes up the story once more.

"While we stood there like dummies, not knowing what to do, the stranger walked through us, singing as he went. In a moment, he was gone."

There is a *snort* from the Code Keeper.

The Teacher ignores it.

"There was nothing left to do but return home. Darkness was falling fast. It was at this point that our fear overtook us. All we wanted, was to get back to the safety of the village and our homes. I confess that we bolted down the trail as if the Hounds of Hades were after us."

Not a soul stirs in the room.

"Now you know the fate of your fathers and all that transpired on the mountain. We need to take these things seriously. What if these strange events and signs are messages from the Divine? What if *he* is the Divine?"

The Code Keeper stares fixedly at the Teacher. His face has turned bright red.

The Teacher removes the gags from the four men. It's only fair that their leaders be able to respond to all they have heard.

CHAPTER 28

"Ah, yes! The Code!"

"Do you take me for a fool?" the Code Keeper bellows. "By the Code, I will have you all soundly flogged until your bones bleed!"

The Teacher is stunned.

"If our fathers fell off a cliff or if there was foul play, then confess it! This stupid story is going to cost you dearly, and you know it!"

The Teacher looks pityingly at the Code Keeper.

"There is none so blind, as those who will not see," he mutters.

The Code Keeper hears him.

"What was that? You call *me* blind? You—a mere teacher, a peddler of numbers and letters. I am the Code Keeper! I am the anointed one! I am..."

"Ah yes, the Code!"

The Teacher stares at the Code Keeper for a few moments.

Everyone knows something is coming and they wait tensely.

Calmly, the Teacher turns to the desk and picks up the sacred book.

"What are you doing?" shouts the horrified Keeper. "It's forbidden!"

The Teacher merely glances at the Keeper and continues opening the book.

Every man in the room holds his breath, expecting either a bolt of lightning or a Divine Agent to strike the Teacher down.

No clap of thunder and no lightning bolt.

Opening at random pages the Teacher begins to read, his eyes skimming quickly over the yellowed pages.

Covering the pages are texts and passages focusing on judgment, death, and destruction. The depressing passages go on and on, spilling out of the pages like dirty water spilling out of a contaminated well.

As the Teacher scans the pages, he sees that something isn't right. He asks the Code Keeper if it is the true Copy.

The Code Keeper turns livid with rage and wants to know what the Teacher is implying?

The Teacher decides he might as well come right out with it.

"There is no coherence to any of these passages or texts. I find it hard to believe it is an exact copy of *anything*!"

The Code Keeper almost chokes, and he rages at the Teacher.

"Are you mad? You'd question something that has been in our care and safe-keeping for generations?"

The Teacher stares down at the pages of the book.

"I *know* there is something wrong here."

"How do you know?" snaps the Keeper.

"I can see it, and I can *feel* it," replies the Teacher quietly.

"Feel it? Perhaps texts have been omitted because they would be wasted on ignorant rabble like you!"

The Code Keeper glares at the men with open contempt on his face. The *ignorant rabble* glare right back.

The Teacher is speaking.

"This *is* the Copy given to the first Code Keeper? The Copy that was written by Divine Agents?"

The Code Keeper huffs through his nose.

"What do you think? You know the history. We have all heard it told enough! *YES*, it is the original Copy of the Code that Divine Agents gave to the first Code Keeper! You can see its age. It has been protected and preserved carefully by *my* predecessors. Why would you question this?"

The Code Keeper decides to try reasoning his way back into control.

"It has been an eventful day. We are all shocked and out of sorts. Why don't you untie us so we can have a calm, rational discussion about your concerns and the matter of the boy! I assume you wish to resolve these issues in a healthy way?"

The Teacher stares knowingly at the Code Keeper. It is when Code Keeper's sound reasonable that you have to watch out.

"We'll sort this out later. We need to take you to the Tree so you can see for yourselves what happened on the mountain."

The Code Keeper gives vent to an exclamation of annoyance. *The dratted man isn't going to be swayed.*

"Keep a firm grip on them," the Teacher orders, "make sure they do not escape."

As the men begin to move, however, the Code Keeper lunges away. The Other three follow suit. Bodies tumble and fall, there is bedlam and confusion.

The Teacher had guessed that the Keeper would try *something*. The instant the Keeper threw himself forwards the Teacher leaped upon him, sending himself and the Code Keeper crashing into the wood paneling of the nearby wall. A loud *'thunk'* and a *'click'* is heard, followed by a rasping sound.

From all around come excited cries and shouts.

The two men pause in their struggles, so they can see what's causing all the fuss. What they see amazes them.

A small panel has moved aside in the wall, revealing a hidden recess. Thick gray dusty cobwebs fill the cavity. There is an odd musty smell. The impact of the two men must have jarred an unknown mechanism, triggering it into action.

"I did not know that was there," calls the Code Keeper. Everyone ignores him. Those who are holding him tighten their grips. Nobody is getting away; nobody is leaving this room.

In the exposed cavity, cobwebs stir slightly in the air. It is clear that the small chamber has not been disturbed for a great length of time.

One of the men brushes the cobwebs away with his whip and gestures for the Teacher to investigate.

The Teacher, with some trepidation, extends his arm into the dark opening. At first, the Teacher cannot feel anything, but as he carefully gropes about, his fingers encounter a couple of bundles. Getting a grip on the items, the Teacher eases them out.

The objects are covered in dust and grime. Both are wrapped in canvas, bound with leather straps and sealed with wax. Stamped deeply into the wax are the letters: *A.S.P.*

The men confer and come to the conclusion that the Founder was the one who hid the objects in the wall cavity. According to the old records, he had undertaken the internal construction of the room himself, refusing all offers of assistance from others.

Someone finds a cloth, and the Teacher wipes away the layers of dust. One of the men hands a knife to him.

The Keeper lets out a sharp cry of protest. "If the Founder hid them, he must have had a good reason!"

Ignoring him, the Teacher carefully slices through the time-hardened leather straps and wax sealing on the first bundle. With great care, he eases back the stiff wrappings.

Papers! Yellowed with age and brittle to the touch. The ink is faded, but it is still possible to read the writing. It is a personal record of the Great Journey, and notes on the establishment of their community. At the top of each page, he sees those initials: *A.S.P.*

Turning to the second bundle, he slowly and carefully peels away the layers. Something different is revealed.

It is a book. A book with a worn black leather cover. On the cover there are letters. However, they are unreadable. It looks like someone has deliberately scratched the letters away, even those down the spine, leaving the book cover in a damaged state.

With every eye in the room upon him, the Teacher opens the book.

Someone has ripped several pages out of the front of the book. The Teacher assumes these would have been title pages. He then sees a long inscription written on the inside of the book's cover. As the Teacher reads what is written, his face turns deathly pale. Shaking his head, he gently closes the book. *How can it be? Is it possible?*

The men can see he is struggling with some deep emotion.

Finally, he holds the old book up so everyone can see it. In a shaking voice, he makes an announcement that leaves every man in the room bereft of speech.

"*This* is the holy black book the Founder carried with him on the Great Journey. It is the black leather-covered book we have heard so much about. It is the *original* Code!"

For the space of a minute, there is silence then the room erupts. Shouts come from every quarter.

"Why would you say that?"

"Nonsense!"

"What proof do you have?" This shout comes from the Code Keeper.

Opening the old book once more, the Teacher reads out the lengthy inscription.

This holy Code is the property of Abraham Silas Pope, First Code Keeper, Founder of the People of the Code.

The room echoes with angry shouts and cries of rage.

The Code Keeper is horrified. His head reels and beads of sweat are on his forehead. It *can't* be the original book. Divine Agents took it into Heaven. The Founder announced it to all the people. Why would he lie? *It has to be a mistake!*

The Code Keeper asks the Teacher if he can see it more closely. The Teacher takes the book over and shows the inscription to the Keeper, who looks at it in sheer disbelief. There's no doubt about it. It can't be anything else. It *is* the Founder's Code.

The Teacher now asks some of the Elders to join him in making a comparison of the Copy and the original Code.

It isn't hard to see that most of the original book has been omitted from the Copy. The original is quite thick, with fine print covering the pages in double columns. The Copy is on thicker parchment paper and the texts written in spidery writing.

The Teacher and the Elders notice reference marks beside the hand-written texts in the Copy. With some searching, they discover where those references are in the original book. It is as the Teacher suspected. The texts have been pulled out at random and given meanings which do not accord with the teaching or theme in the original book.

The Elders and the Teacher look at each other with grim faces.

Next, they compare the writing in the Copy with the writing in the journal notes, and their suspicions are confirmed.

The Teacher and the Elders are sickened. They turn away, refusing to make eye contact with the Code Keeper who is wanting to know what they have discovered.

The Teacher snatches up the Copy and shakes it angrily, in the Code Keeper's face.

"Your so-called Copy is a fake! It's nothing more than texts and passages pulled at random from the original. It's not a real copy at all. As for being written by Divine Agents, that's a lie as well! The Copy was written by the Founder; this *Abraham Silas Pope.*"

He flings the Copy across the room. It hits the wall and drops to the floor.

Shock registers on every face.

The Code Keeper feels the ground shift under his feet.

A Carpenter yells, "So *everything* is a lie! There were *no* Divine Agents. The Founder's black book was *not* taken into heaven, and the Copy is a fake, written by a man called, *Abraham Silas Pope*. Am I correct? Have I got it right so far?"

"But why? Why would the Founder deceive everyone like that?" someone shouts.

One of the Elder's responds.

"Why? It's obvious, man! By keeping the original Code hidden, nobody would know that the Copy was a false one. He apparently picked texts that fit in with his beliefs, rejecting everything that didn't! Which in this case, appears to be almost *all* of the original book!"

The Tailor elbows his way forward, shouting angrily.

"Haven't we wondered? Haven't we questioned in our minds?"

He glares at the pale Code Keeper.

"Let's put an end to this cruel regime and its lies, once and for all."

There are loud choruses of "Amen," from every quarter.

The four bound men wisely keep quiet. Besides, what *can* they say? The foundations of their existence have just been swept away in a landslide of exposure and revelation.

The Blacksmith picks up the Copy from the floor.

"What do you want to do with this?"

"We'll toss it into the Burning. That's all the miserable book is good for," snaps one of the Elders.

The Code Keeper nearly faints when he hears this. *Why did this have to happen on his watch?* He sighs deeply. There is no denying the facts. The proof is right there in front of them.

Someone asks the Teacher to read out a text from the original black book.

Opening up at a random page, the Teacher reads the following passage.

> *Let them praise his name in the dance; let them sing praises unto him with the timbrel and harp.*[5]

"Timbrels and dancing? Really? I love it!" shouts the Tailor. "Keep reading!"

The Teacher smiles and moves on to another text.

> *For the LORD taketh pleasure in his people; he will beautify the meek with salvation. Let the saints be joyful in glory; let them sing aloud upon their beds.*[6]

The room fills with animated conversation.

The Leatherman speaks up.

"No wonder the Founder hid the original Code. These texts are full of life, not the stinking doom and gloom that he and Code Keepers have been shoving down our throats!"

One of the Woodsmen speaks.

"If the 'Lord' mentioned in those texts, is God himself, then he is a very different God to the God of the Founder. *This* God enjoys his people."

The Teacher opens up to another section, more towards the front of the book. As he scans the page, his blood runs cold. His eye has caught a verse that is listed among what appear to be, several moral laws.

Thou shalt not kill.[7]

The Code Keeper's eyes bulge. *Not kill? But...!*

He thinks of how Code Keepers have dealt with intruders, trouble-makers and those who were unwanted. He thinks of the Tree, the Exile, and other punishments. Then, with a shudder, he thinks of their Law of Age!

The Code Keeper is now visibly shaking from head to foot. He looks so terrible that the men wonder if he is going to have a collapse of some kind.

"Who gave that command?" the terrified Keeper asks, in a shaking voice.

The Teacher looks at the preceding texts.

And God spoke all these words...[8]

An awful cry erupts from the Code Keeper. His head drops. His voice is a mere whisper.

"Don't read any more, for pity's sake."

The Teacher isn't feeling too good himself. The command, given by God, means that the conscious, deliberate taking of life is murder. *Murder!* His mind reels. He ponders the command and all of its implications.

He is not the only one.

Every face has gone pale. Some of the men gaze upwards, anguish evident on their faces. Others have covered their face with their hands, an awful pain of guilt suddenly washing over them.

As if scales have fallen from their eyes, the men see what they have not seen before. Light is shining into their darkened minds and what they see is not only horrifying, it is devastating!

"What are we to do?" cries one of the Weavers. "God will surely punish us now. We are all going to be destroyed in Fiery Judgment."

The Teacher feels an inner prompting to open the book again at another place. It falls open at a book written by a man named 'John.'

> *For God so loved the world, that he gave his only begotten Son, that whosoever believeth in him should not perish, but have everlasting life.*[9]

The Teacher reads the words out, and as he does, a shock thrills his soul. He reads the words out again, louder this time.

"What is this saying?" someone calls out. "We can escape Fiery Judgment? God has a son? What are we hearing here?"

The Teacher, still following some inner prompting, turns the pages back to a section called 'Luke.' He skims over several of the pages, before looking around the room full of men.

"You are going to love what is written here."

The Teacher finds his cheeks are wet with tears. As if someone is guiding his hand, he turns to a book titled 'Isaiah.' What he reads, produces even more tears.

> *The Spirit of the LORD GOD is upon me, because the LORD hath anointed me to preach good tidings unto the meek; he hath sent me to bind up the brokenhearted, to proclaim liberty to the captives, and the opening of the prison to those who are bound.*[10]

One of the Elders brushes at his own eyes with his hands and speaks up in a trembling voice.

"I have always wondered about the God of the Founder. How could the Founder portray God the way he did? A cruel, heartless, vengeful Being, who cared only about inflicting pain and torment. It just didn't seem to ring true. There were times when I struggled to believe in a God at all."

One of the Growers now speaks.

"These words are telling us that the 'Lord God' sends *good* tidings and wants to bind up broken hearts. He wants to declare freedom to people in captivity and open the prisons of those who are bound. The Founder's religious beliefs have done the total opposite! These words apply to us! I want to know more about this God!"

The Keeper has pushed through his pain. He speaks out, and he does not couch his words.

"Forget about the God of the Founder. He's clearly a God *created* by the Founder himself; this *Abraham Silas Pope*. It seems to me that he gave God his *own* qualities and shaped *his* God in his *own image*."

The men hear what he is saying and nod. They can see what the Keeper is saying. The Elder gives a quiet "Amen."

The Keeper isn't finished.

"We now have the original black book, and as the Teacher says, I think we should look to *that* for answers. Forget the teachings of the Founder and us Code Keepers. Everything that's been passed on to us has been a lie. I cannot carry this rotten burden. I *refuse* to!"

The Code Keeper sighs deeply and rubs his eyes.

"I'm just as affected by all of this, as you are! Don't you think I questioned my father about our laws and protocols? I did, and was always flogged for it. If you don't believe me, I will show you."

He removes his jacket and lifts his shirt, turning so that his back is to the room.

The men are appalled by what they see. The young Code Keeper's back is covered in ugly raised scars and welts. They'd thought the Code Keeper tough on *them,* however, it appears that he was far more zealous in what he inflicted upon his son.

The young man pulls down his shirt, covering himself up.

"If you think my father was heavy-handed with me, I can assure you that he was much harder in his treatment of my sister."

Every eye looks at the Teacher, who coughs and looks down at the floor. He shudders with shame as he thinks of the times he has added injury to the ones she has already suffered. All in the name of "discipline." *What's wrong with us men? Are we that insecure, that we must hurt and cripple our women?*

The other men shuffle and shift, uncomfortable with what the young Code Keeper has revealed.

Can there possibly be any more revelations?

Is there anything else that is going to leave them reeling?

The Carpenter pushes forward until he is standing directly in front of the Code Keeper.

"I'm sure every man in this room wants to ask this question. Was there a Fiery Judgment?"

Before the Keeper has a chance to answer, there is a loud "Hah" from the back of the room.

Heads turn.

It is the Traveler. He pushes his way forward.

"*I* will be the one to answer this!"

Both the Keeper and the Healer start to say something. However, the Traveler cuts them off.

"You will not silence me," he rumbles. "Our kind have been silent for far too long."

(The men are amazed to see the Traveler there. How did he know what was happening? Who told him?)

The Traveler looks around the room, his gaze passing over the face of every man.

"There was *no* Fiery Judgment from God."

All hell breaks loose in the crowded room.

CHAPTER 29

Deceiver, Murderer.

He stands among the gathered men, his Presence unseen and his singing unheard.

Healing can only take place when infected wounds are opened, and the poison dealt with.

Gently, his music reveals the infection and draws the poison out...

The Traveler bellows for everyone to be quiet! He has more to say, and they'd better listen.

"Life goes on. Towns and villages grow. Farming communities are spreading. The world below has changed, but it has *not* been destroyed."

Fury fills the hearts of the men as they realize that here is yet another exposed lie.

"The so-called *Fiery Judgment* that destroyed our ancestors' town was in fact, a fire set by the Founder's *own* hand for personal reasons."

He pauses, chewing on his lip.

"There is something else. I've heard the name, *Abraham Silas Pope* before."

The Traveler heard many things during his travels. Some things he remembered. Some he forgot.

Janice Mau

When the Teacher read out the name, *Abraham Silas Pope,* it triggered a memory; a memory of an evening spent with an old farmer, who had lived down on the plains.

The farmer had invited him in for a meal. As they'd sat by the fire, the old man had shared that he was the sole surviving member of a family, whose ancestors had lived in a town that suffered a terrible tragedy.

The old man had pulled over a battered wooden box in which there were papers and documents. Removing a worn, stained envelope, the farmer had handed it to the Traveler. He'd explained that it was a letter written by his ancestor who'd lived in that town. He had found the letter in the box, which itself had been hidden, jammed up against the stonework of the chimney. He'd discovered it while repairing some floor timbers.

The Traveler had opened the envelope and read its contents.

The author began by explaining that he had a confession to make and would the reader forgive him if it was overly long.

The author shared that he'd once been a hotel owner in a particular town. Late one night he had accepted a sizeable bribe from a member of a wealthy family, who were in the practice of using an upstairs room as a private meeting room. In exchange for handing over the keys of the hotel, the author had received a wooden box containing bags of gold and silver coins. The hotel hadn't been doing well. The money had been too much to resist.

The gentleman had instructed the author to leave the premises and say nothing. There would be dire consequences if he did, and the man had threatened the author with a horsewhip. A horsewhip which, the author remembered, had a beautiful silver handle.

Despite the man's warnings, the author had hidden where he could observe the man's actions. To his surprise, the gentleman had gone upstairs and locked the door of the room in which the rest of his family were gathered. After this, he'd gone back downstairs and into the storeroom, which happened to be directly below the upstairs room.

Inside the storeroom, the man had opened barrels of paraffin oil and splashed the contents everywhere. He then set fire to the goods in the storeroom. When the room was a raging inferno, the man had run out the back of the hotel. His family remained trapped in the upstairs room.

The author confessed that when he had heard the cries and screams coming from upstairs, he had panicked and run. He'd hidden the box in his home before running off to the authorities with a tale of intruders and arsonists. His story had been believed. The fire was deemed a tragedy.

The author had never spoken with the gentleman again, and he'd kept his promise to maintain secrecy.

Out of curiosity, the author had kept an eye on the man, even followed him now and then. He had wanted to see what else the man might get up to.

The author went on to say that the gentleman had become a problem in the town due to constantly harassing the town's residents about their wicked ways. One night, after being tossed into a horse-trough, the man had raged home, loaded a wagon and set fire to his house. When the house was a raging inferno, the man had mounted his wagon and headed out of town at a fast gallop.

Seeing that the terrible fire was spreading, the author had rushed to his own home to save his family and anything he could. The author had packed the box of coins in the wagon first.

They had headed south, and he had used some of the bribe money to purchase the land and build a comfortable home. They'd enjoyed a good life for some years.

The author wrote that his wife and two of his four sons had contracted an illness and died. He hoped that his remaining children would fare better.

Not wanting to depart this world with unconfessed sins, he'd decided to write his crime down. However, being a coward, he would be hiding the letter, and he hoped it would not be discovered until well after his death.

As a footnote, the writer had added that the name of the arsonist (slash) murderer, was *Abraham Silas Pope*.

When the Traveler had finished reading the lengthy missive the old man had taken the letter from him in shaking hands and cast it into the fire.

The Traveler had thanked the old man for his hospitality, wished him well and taken his leave.

The Traveler had recognized the town in the letter. It was the one their Founder and ancestors had come from, the one on which Fiery Judgment had supposedly fallen.

As the Traveler had continued his travels, he had mulled over the letter's contents, appalled at what the letter had revealed. Then with one thing or another, the matter slipped his mind *until* the Teacher read the inscription in the discovered book.

The Traveler passes all of this information on to the crowd of stunned listeners, who have been absorbing every single word. Before returning to his place at the back of the crowd, he says one last thing.

"*Abraham Silas Pope*! Founder and first Code Keeper. Deceiver and murderer. That is the truth. What will you do with it?"

Chapter 30

Facing the Truth

He is standing among them, his heart overflowing with compassion. He knows that the Other is also listening, hoping for further pain and tragedy.

The singer smiles. He will work, and who shall hinder him? Certainly not an enemy who is already defeated!

Humming softly, the singer covers the crowd of hurting, angry men with a canopy of grace.

Their long awaited miracle is close at hand.

Nobody dares speak. All they have heard, is a cataclysmic event, turning their lives upside down. An event that is leaving them stunned, dazed, and in shock.

Mercilessly, the Teacher continues.

"Our entire existence, as the people of the Code, is a lie and has been from the very beginning. Didn't any of our ancestors think to question? Were they that beaten into submission that they lost the ability to reason; to think for themselves? I shudder to think of what it took for the Founder to get the people into such a passive and accepting state."

One of the Elders speaks up.

"Why do you say that? All it took was the same methods that our leaders apply today! Intimidation, and keeping people in thrall to fear. We are no different to our ancestors."

Heads turn, and all eyes fasten on the four leaders. The contrite and penitent Code Keeper included. From every corner of the room come demands that the four leaders be taken to the nearest tree and hung.

The four men are terrified.

Some of the men begin to push and prod the four leaders. A few manage to deliver resounding blows with clenched fists. Bodies surge backward and forwards as some try to drag the four men out for 'justice,' while others try to prevent it.

The situation is explosive.

In desperation, the four men turn pleading eyes to the Teacher. He sees their fear, yet can't help thinking how quickly the tables have turned. Those who have traditionally never shown mercy to others are now looking for mercy to be shown to *them*.

Despite his anger, the Teacher doesn't want to start a new life on a foundation of violence. That's what the old regime had been built on, and the results have been nothing but pain and joyless living.

He raises his hands, shouting loudly to get the men's attention.

"Stop! Stop what you are doing! If we murder these four men, we are no different to their fathers or the Founder. I, for one, have no desire to begin my new life, with blood on my hands!"

The Hunter shouts angrily.

"Why are you trying to stop us? You are the one who raced around, knocking on our doors, telling us that the time had come to put an end to things. Why are you showing weakness? We have to see this thing through to the end."

One of the Weavers shouts his support of the Hunter.

"We can't make a new start if these four men are a part of it. At some point, they'll turn everything back to the way it was. We can't afford to let them live!"

Emotions are boiling over again.

As things reach crisis point, the Teacher hears four words blast through his mind: *"Thou shalt not kill!"*

He puts his hand up to his head. The words had been so loud that he'd almost *felt* them. Could it be the same voice that spoke to his wife? If so...

He grabs the precious Code and climbs onto the desktop, scattering parchments everywhere. Standing above the seething crowd of men, he thunders:

"Thou shalt not kill!"

Raised fists freeze in mid-action. Bodies go still. All noise and argument cease. Eyes stare in shock at the man standing on the desktop, holding the black book aloft, his face fierce and determined.

The Teacher repeats the text in an even louder voice, emphasizing every word.

"God says, in the true Code, "Thou shalt not kill!""

The men stand undecided for a moment, then those who had demanded justice, back down. They look at each other, then at their raised fists and horsewhips.

They suddenly see how close they have come to being the very people they have wanted to destroy. *We are no different,* is the thought that now fills many minds. The thought terrifies them.

Someone calls out, asking *why* the four men should not receive *some* punishment?

The Teacher steps back down from the desk and reminds them in no uncertain terms that none of *them* is innocent. He points to the four men, who are slumped in the chairs with the evidence of blows, on their faces.

"Didn't we accompany their fathers when they took the stranger to the Tree? Did we try to stop what was happening? Did we make *any* protest?"

The men shift uncomfortably.

"Because they *remove* those who do!"

It is one of the Hunters, and he is still fuming.

"I know that!" responds the Teacher. "But we need to understand that they've only been obeying laws that were *imprinted* on them by others."

He sighs deeply.

"This Code Keeper only knows what he has been taught. The same goes for the rest of us. So who do we punish? In a way, we've all had *no choice* in how we've acted."

The ears of the *Other* prick up. Now *that's* interesting. The Teacher is sliding into *justification*.

The *Other* stretches luxuriously. There are times when it could almost love their pathetic human nature.

It ponders for a second.

"Meh!"

While the Teacher is still speaking, one of the Elders steps up, and his face is stern.

"What you say, is *not* entirely accurate!"

He scans the faces of the crowd.

"Within every person, there is a conscience. There is a built-in knowledge, *instinct*, if you will, which prods us when we contemplate committing a wrong against another. Yes, we have all been taught a certain way, but I challenge each and every one of you, to *deny* that you have felt a *wrongness* every time you raised a whip, cruel words were spoken, or death was meted out. I challenge you...as I challenge myself."

The Teacher heaves a sigh.

"The Elder is right. If we can't face the truth, then we may as well go home and forget about a new life."

(The *Other* snarls in exasperation. Damn that Elder. Always some righteous do-gooder stepping up and spoiling things.)

The Teacher continues.

"I have to confess, that on the occasions I disciplined my wife or son with the horsewhip, I have felt something cry out deep inside, as if a hand was raised in protest, or a voice was calling out "Stop." I always chose to ignore it."

He looks down.

"My so-called *manly* pride."

Many of the men are nodding in agreement, hearing the Teacher's words and taking them to heart.

The Code Keeper has heard enough. It's over, finished. *He's finished!*

He's tried to be a Code Keeper, and even gone to lengths to be tougher than his father; for what purpose? Why? He'd hated their laws and protocols, even as a boy, and no matter how cruelly his father disciplined him, he'd always carried doubts in his heart. He is finally glad to be able to admit it. His father had always feared that "a weak son" would undo the work of the Founder. This is why his father had disciplined him so vigorously over the years. It is ironic that his father's fears are now being realized.

The Code Keeper gives a painful laugh, then squares his shoulders and addresses the crowded room.

"So, this is it! The original black book has been found. The book we've all been trained to obey turns out to be a lie. We have done things which are in complete opposition to what God himself says in his written word, the true Code."

He stares around the room, nodding, as if to himself.

"I am the *last* Code Keeper of the people of the Code. Who'd have thought?"

The men in the room are silent. What they have hoped and longed for is coming to pass. Are they dreaming? Some pinch themselves just to make sure.

The Code Keeper turns to the other three men, who have not said a word. They have wanted to see how things turn out. To be honest, they were also afraid to say anything, in case they reaped a harsh response from the Code Keeper, or the room full of angry men.

They listen to what the Code Keeper is saying.

"Our time is over. The old ways cannot continue. *We* cannot continue. We either embrace the changes that are coming, or we must leave. Whatever we do, there will no longer be a reign of Code Keepers, enforcing cruel laws upon the people."

He steps to one side of the room and nods at the Teacher.

"Teacher; you, the Elders and the people can plan for the future from this point on."

The Code Keeper looks over at the Healer and two Stalwarts.

"Do you three have anything to say? You must have some thoughts of your own, surely?"

The Healer speaks first.

"I can only speak for myself when I say, that it horrifies me, that I've been doing what is in complete opposition to the true Code. I cannot understand it. Is it possible to become so hardened that one is unable to hear the *inner voice,* the Elder spoke about? But getting back to your question: if you still want me to be Healer, then that is what I will be. I am willing to work in with whatever decisions you make."

He turns to the Stalwarts. "What about you two?"

The Stalwarts look helplessly at those around them. One of them finds his voice.

"You ask us? As Stalwarts, we are not used to thinking for ourselves. All we know is how to obey the commands, "do this" or "do that." We've followed orders our entire lives. If you are willing to let us stay, then I guess we can make changes too, but we'll need help in adjusting."

The Other Stalwart decides to speak up.

"I know that you would all like to toss us out of the village. I know some of you want to string us up on the Tree. You'd have every right to do so. We have followed orders to inflict pain. I don't know how we can fit into a new beginning, but I guess we'll find out. Sorry, that's about all I can say."

The men have been listening to the Stalwarts with surprise on their faces and their mouths hanging open. Unbelievably, some of them start to grin. One or two even chuckle.

The Stalwarts look around, puzzled. What? What did they say that was funny?

The Code Keeper is looking at them with stunned amazement on his face.

"I didn't know you two had that many words in your vocabulary."

A shout of laughter comes from the back of the room. It is the Traveler.

He's not the only one breaking into laughter.

The Keeper's comment has acted as a catalyst.

Men who have never laughed in their lives are breaking out into loud guffaws and hoots of laughter. It's as if all the suppressed pain, stress and fear is being released in a flood of laughter. They could no more stop it than they could stop a rampaging bear.

The Healer and Stalwarts are astounded. *What is this?* A few moments ago they were in fear for their lives. The Stalwarts shake their heads. *We don't understand.*

CHAPTER 31

Miracle of Life

His heart rejoices. Laughter is powerful when it is pure and clean. Laughter can effect great release and healing and is a weapon of strength. Laughter is a powerful part of rejoicing. The word 'Rejoice' itself has significant meaning: to spin or dance wildly in high emotion. Yes, laughter is a beautiful releasing gift he has given humanity, and it bears rich fruit when it flows clean and free.

He weaves among the men in the room, who are shouting and laughing, tears streaming down their faces.

Like a wind of rainbow colors, his Song sweeps through the room working its miracle.

The men lean on one another, wiping their eyes. They feel as if they have just climbed to the peaks and back several times.

They marvel at what has just happened. It is as if a mighty river has roared through their souls, pushing all the rubbish and dead things before it. They feel clean and new as if they have just been born.

They look at the Teacher expectantly.

The Teacher stares back with raised eyebrows.

One of the Elders smiles. "Teacher, what do you suggest we do next?"

"Why are you all looking at me? I'm not a leader. I have no *authority.*"

The Code Keeper grins broadly.

"Oh, I wouldn't say that, Teacher. You've done pretty well so far, including standing on my desk! (More shouts of laughter.) Besides, this *new* path we are about to venture on requires someone new."

It is not what the Teacher wants, considering he has shown himself to be a weak man not that long ago. However, if this is what everyone wants?

Everyone assures him that it is. They give the Teacher loud assurances that they will work with him and alongside him in the days ahead.

He straightens up, feeling overwhelmed, yet nodding acceptance. *Things are certainly going to be different. It will take a lot of joint work and effort, but it will all be worth it.*

"Right now, I feel we need to get to the Tree. I'm not sure why. It's just what I feel."

The men are happy to follow his suggestion, and they follow him out of the building.

To their amazement, they find their families waiting outside, even the school students. Wonder, bewilderment, joy and tears are on many faces.

(The sound of the men's laughter had carried to every building in the village. Wondering what was going on, families had come out of their homes and approached the Great House. Students had left the schoolhouse and joined them.)

When the men see their families and the joy on their faces, their hearts feel close to bursting. The power that moved upon *them* has moved upon their families.

The Teacher manages to make himself heard above all the talking and laughter. He announces that they are going to the Tree and everyone is welcome to come.

It is a very different procession to the last one.

As the people pass through the fields, children run to and fro, chasing each other around the adults and in and out of the surrounding fields. The air rings with the sound of their happy laughter and playful shouting.

The Traveler is running along the plateau, to fetch his wife. His son is playing with the other children. He isn't worried about missing out on anything. The way the people are chatting and enjoying the walk, there will be plenty of time for them to catch up.

The Traveler is right. The people are taking a keen interest in just about everything. Especially the wildflowers that grow in abundance. Children run backward and forwards picking flowers, bringing them to their mothers.

The Teacher's wife cannot believe what is happening. Not long ago she was being exiled for hiding small flowers; now everyone is permitted to enjoy them freely. Her son presents her with a pretty bouquet, and she hugs him, laughing merrily.

Heads are spinning at what is taking place. Most of them half expect the Code Keeper to start shouting or the Stalwarts to start barking orders. However, the young Code Keeper is enjoying their surroundings as much as anyone else. As for the horsewhip *Righteousness,* there is no sign of it, or of any other horsewhip. They have been left behind.

It is little details like this that show a great change has occurred. The happy villagers have no doubt that in the coming days they are going to see many others.

As for the Teacher; he is leading the merry procession, his wife, and son alongside him. There is a sense of *rightness* about what is happening.

He is also carrying the precious black book. It has been wrapped in a cloth to protect it for it is now the most valuable asset in their community. They will need to make copies, or perhaps the Traveler could see if others are in existence, when he makes his journey to the lands below.

At this thought, the Teacher feels a sense of excitement. Maybe he and some others could go too? Why not? *Oh, we are in for some wonderful times.*

Finally, the villagers emerge onto the broad ledge high up on the escarpment slopes, and there they see the blackened ruined remains of the Tree.

Noisy chatter and laughter cease. Children hide behind their parents. Even they can sense the evil that has been done there.

The Teacher and the men look about the blackened area cautiously. Surprisingly, there is no sign of the bodies of their former leaders. The men heave sighs of relief.

It is the first time that *these* four leaders have made this particular journey. Since stepping into their father's roles, they have had no cause to bring anyone here themselves, and are now *very* glad of it.

A loud cry echoes overhead and every eye looks up. A magnificent eagle is circling above them. They watch the aerial display for a few moments, before turning their gaze back to the Tree.

A collective gasp goes up.

It is the boy! He is standing beside the ruined stump.

The people stare at the young fellow. He looks the same, but there is *something else.*

The boy smiles and beckons them closer. As they crowd around him, he turns and places his hands on the blackened, ruined trunk of the Tree.

A beautiful song pours from his lips.

From deep within the ruined trunk, the people see a tender young shoot sprouting up. Delicate and green, it reaches toward the light, stretching, growing, green leaves appearing one by one. The shoot rises upwards, tendrils unfurling and leaves opening. Soon it is a sapling, then quickly it grows from a sapling into a sturdy tree. As the boy continues singing, the young tree keeps growing.

The people step back, in awe at the miracle occurring before their eyes.

The old ruined trunk crumbles away.

A tall giant with broad spreading branches and a dense canopy of leaves is standing in its place.

The people gaze at the new tree in astonishment. It is covered in brightly colored flowers; flowers that ripple and shift. Flowers that quickly reveal themselves to be jewel-bright butterflies—the *same* butterflies that had flown into the schoolroom.

A long sigh is heard as if it has come from the Tree itself. The kind of sigh one makes when arriving home from a long, tiring journey. It is a sigh of joy and relief.

The clearing itself has changed. Green grass now carpets the area and wildflowers add texture and contrast with their bright colors.

The boy's song finishes, and he straightens up. Only he is a boy no longer; he is the stranger—the stranger in the long cloak. A cloak that is now dancing and rippling with every color and shade imaginable; a cloak that gently undulates and flows of its own accord.

The people gaze at the stranger in wonder. *Who is this person?*

The stranger's eyes move over the silent crowd, and his heart thrums with compassion.

(Dear humanity! In the Beginning, he had lovingly created man and woman, filled them with the music of life and placed them in a beautiful environment he had prepared just for them. Their home had been one of rare beauty, and their life had been a song of peace, laughter, love and purpose. Above all, they had enjoyed a close bond with him and learned to sing with him. They could have lived forever.

Then the Devourer, the *Other*, insinuated its melody into their lives. A song designed to steal and destroy the music he had given them, the music within them. If only they had not succumbed to that deadly song. For *deadly* it is.

The stranger smiles gently.

This is why he will continue singing and weaving his music—to bring release, healing, and restoration of what was stolen from his children in that garden.)

The sound of air rushing through wings is heard, and the eagle alights on a branch of the Tree.

The stranger looks up at the eagle, which stretches its head toward him in an attitude of inquiry.

"Do you forgive them?"

"Oh, I already did that a long time ago," is the soft response.

The great bird chitters in its throat and tilts its head.

"Will you teach them, give them your Name, your Song?"

The eagle's companion smiles.

"Yes! Many are going to accept my Song into their hearts! To them, I will give my Name."

He turns a radiant smile upon the people standing nervously about him.

It is the Teacher who raises his hand and in a hesitant voice asks the stranger the question that is in every mind.

"Who are you?"

The stranger turns and indicates the Tree, which is standing tall and proud, with colorful butterflies dancing among its leaves.

"*There* is the evidence of who I am, and what I do."

The people stare at the beautiful tree—recreated, born again; raised up out of the ruined stump, and adorned with beauty.

He looks at the Teacher, with a warm smile on his face and light dancing in his eyes.

"You are going to enjoy reading the letters of my friends. Begin with Luke's, then read John's. Study the whole book, Teacher. Share everything with the people, young and old. It is not just for leaders; it is for every soul."

The Teacher clutches the book close. His heart feels like it is going to explode with joy.

A loud shout echoes round the clearing.

It is the Traveler. (He's always shouting.) He is pushing his way forward in great excitement.

"It's *you*, isn't it? *You're* the one who created all things. *You're* the Creator!"

The Creator nods and laughs happily.

"Dear Traveler, how I love our conversations. Did you enjoy our brief adventure in the snow, among the wolves?"

The Traveler's son, who is nearby, leaps into the air with a loud whoop.

"I knew it! Didn't I tell you? I *knew* it was him."

Red-faced, the Traveler turns toward everyone and promises he will tell them about it later.

The day is passing, and the sun is beginning its descent below the ridgeline.

The Creator gestures toward the new Tree.

"If you are willing, I will sing for *you*. My Song will be a spring of living water deep in your spirit; a Song that will bring healing, restoration, and new life. The more you choose to drink from my Song, the more it will flow."

He smiles warmly at every soul standing in the clearing. "The choice is yours, and yours alone."

The people look at the giant Tree then look at each other. Many have huge grins on their faces as they contemplate the miracle being offered to them.

The Blacksmith can't wait and yells out.

"Oh for goodness sake, what are you all waiting for?"

As if the Blacksmith's voice was a trumpet call, the people crowd forward, excitement and *expectation* in their hearts.

The Creator sees the eagerness in the people's hearts and laughs, his joy overflowing. Stretching his arms wide, he gathers them around him, like a hen gathering her chicks.

Creation becomes hushed.

In the Heavens, there is silence as Angels bend to listen.

On the high rocky ledge, below the beautiful towering Tree, the Creator begins to sing...

Book II

There is no place where his Song is not heard...

She tucks the blankets in around the old man. He smiles up at her.

"Have you heard anything?"

His voice is frail and weak, like his body.

"No grandpa, I haven't. I'm sorry."

She knows what he is referring to.

It's time for her to go. Her grandfather won't let her stay, as he hates being fussed over. As she leaves, she turns, knowing what she will see. Her grandfather will be lying in such a way, that he can keep an eye on the door. He wants it left open. Always open.

"Just in case," is all he says when she asks why.

The woman heads off to her home.

Pale moonlight streams in through the open door of the old timber cottage, painting the floor and door frame in silver.

The old man shifts, trying to get more comfortable. His body aches. The pain doesn't let up for a second. Closing his eyes, he lets his mind drift.

He's the last of those known only by their work title. After the Change, he could have given himself a new name, but he hadn't wanted to.

The old man sighs deeply.

He must be well over one hundred years old by now. He's lost count. The years have blended. They are all a blur.

A sound breaks in on the old man's musings.

He opens his eyes.

A figure is standing in the doorway; a figure who is wearing a long cloak, with moonlight, stars, and shadows dancing in its rippling folds.

"Hello, Teacher, have you been waiting long?"

There is a smile in the voice.

The old man lets out a crackle of laughter, and his eyes fill with tears. He tries to speak, but all he can do is smile, his wrinkled face alight with joy.

His visitor laughs softly. Stepping forward, he gently takes the frail, withered hands in his own.

"Come on, old friend. It's time we sang together, you and I…"

The wind blows wherever it pleases. You hear its sound, but you cannot tell where it comes from or where it is going. So it is with everyone born of the Spirit.[11]

CHAPTER 32

Roses in the Outback

In a land of blue skies, red bull-dust, kangaroos, and cockatoos, a frail elderly woman sits in a rocking chair on the verandah of a little outback home.

She gazes out at the red dust and straggly clumps of tussock grass. Shrubs and a few tall Eucalypts break the starkness of the scene.

Desert country...true outback.

She has always loved it.

Her gnarled hands caress the ends of the rocker's wooden arms, and her heart thumps strangely as she lets her mind drift back to early days; days that now seem distant dreams... all flickering shadows in a mist.

She and her parents had not been born in this country. They had come here from another, on the far side of the world. The outback landscape had been such a contrast to their former home—a high plateau surrounded by rugged peaks and ridgelines. A beautiful place. Families like her own had been living in that mountain community since its founding a very long time ago.

The old woman smiles.

Her family were originally known as the *Teacher* family.

Her mother once told her that way back then; nobody used names. They had been known only by a title which denoted their role in the community.

After something called the *Change*, first names were added, drawing on names from a Bible the villagers had.

The old woman nods to herself.

Apparently, the book had been called *the Code*. The people hadn't known it was called a *Bible*.

In later times, the surname *Teacher* had been considered unusual. However, the family would not change it, for it carried their history within it. When she married, of course, her last name changed. However, she still tended to think of herself as *Ruth Teacher*.

Her mother had passed on a great many things, but now she can't recall that much. However, she does vaguely remember something about a singing stranger who worked a miracle in the lives of the people.

The old woman looks down, smoothing her apron.

Faded and wrinkled, just like me.

Rocking back and forth, she looks at the sagging verandah railings, seeing the worn places where her husband Dusty used to sling his saddle and gear at the end of a day's work.

The rose bushes in front of the verandah have become big, straggly and overgrown but they are still covered with heavy-headed roses whose perfume fills the air.

The old woman's eyes mist. Everything around her holds memories. She dabs at her eyes with the corner of her faded apron and falls back into her day dreaming.

A tremulous smile appears on the wrinkled face. The old woman remembers how she and her husband met.

Chapter 33

Dusty

It hadn't been difficult making new friends in the small outback school. The other children were keen to be friends with a new girl. They enjoyed listening to her accent, and many laughs were had at her expense. All of it in good fun and humor.

Dusty had been one of the older boys. He used to laugh at her accent and call her "Lah-dee-dah."

Dusty's home had been a large cattle property many miles away, so he had boarded with family friends who ran the local hotel. She had liked his cheeky smile, blue eyes, and fair hair.

He had been called *Dusty* for the simple reason that he always seemed to be dusty, no matter how hard he brushed at the clinging red dust before entering the school building.

What had caught her attention, was the cute little tune he was always humming or whistling. Nobody had known the name of the theme. Oddly enough, neither had Dusty. So it was merely referred to as *his* song.

She had finished her schooling at a Girls' Boarding school, called *The Sisters of Saint Bertha* (or something like that, she can't remember). After that, she had taken up working in the General Store with her parents.

Dusty had gone home to work on his father's vast cattle station.

She had always looked forward to the times when Dusty came to town. He would come into their shop for supplies, whistling his tune as he entered.

If she were in the back sorting out stock, she would stop what she was doing and race through to exchange a few words with him.

There used to be dances held once a month in the town's community hall. Everyone would go. The dance was the highlight of their lives. People would arrive from all over the place, and it would be a great night.

There would be the inevitable fist fights after some had had a few too many drinks, but, all in all, the dance nights went well.

She had loved those dance nights and loved the raggedy band which belted out old tunes, as well as popular songs of the day. Usually off-key and quite often getting the words wrong, especially after a few beers, but nobody cared.

It was at one of these dances that Dusty had approached her with a serious look on his face, asking her to dance with him. It hadn't been the first time they'd danced together, and they had always indulged in friendly banter on those occasions, but something had been different that night.

The band had started up a slow waltz, and as she stepped into his arms, her heart had flipped strangely. She had given a start, and so had he. Next thing, they had been swept along with the crowd, moving around the dance floor but they may as well have been in the middle of the desert; they had only been aware of each other. When the music stopped, they had gone outside to sit on the balcony steps.

The moon had been shining. An enormous glowing ball in the sky, painting everything in pale, silvery light.

Music, laughter, people and light had spilled out through the open doors, but she and Dusty had been oblivious.

It had been the most natural thing in the world to lean her head on his chest and for his arms to wrap around her. He had begun to hum his tune, and she had loved how she could feel the vibration of his humming in his chest.

His song became *their* song.

They were married and moved out to the small timber and corrugated iron home, on the fringe of the central desert. There had been music in her heart and music in their marriage.

The music had fallen silent a long time ago.

CHAPTER 34

Dinner sets and Kimonos

Dusty! Her heart cries, the familiar ache making its presence felt.

He had often gone away to inspect fence lines or work with the cattle. He would be gone for several days. When he was home, he would fix things up and build this or that. There had always been something to do.

They had a radio through which they would order goods and supplies. Mail Order catalogs had been the thing. Their orders and supplies were always trucked in.

She didn't order much now apart from basics. She didn't need much more than that.

The visit of the trucks had always been an event, a chance to catch up on news and gossip. The driver and his helper would stay a while, chatting over a huge pot of tea and scones. It was always hard to see them go, red dust billowing behind them. A month or more would pass before they saw the truck again unless it was important mail, then an extra trip out would be made.

Her parents had given her a treadle sewing machine and bolts of fabric when she and Dusty married, so she had been able to pretty up the place with curtains, tablecloths, and such.

Dusty had laughed and swung her around, praising her efforts. It hadn't bothered him that the curtains were at odd lengths or the tablecloth was big enough to "cover the Rock" (as he would say).

Her Dusty was always laughing. If he weren't laughing, he would be whistling or humming their tune.

Dusty had built a frame for a garden bed, and they had had some bags of good soil trucked in. They had mixed some of the cattle manure in with it, and soon she had a vegetable garden established.

She also used to order books which taught how to propagate plants and other useful skills.

They had needed to be as self-sufficient as possible.

The old woman twists a corner of her apron and sighs deeply.

She fell pregnant three times, but each time she had miscarried. There were three little crosses under a tall Gumtree out the back.

Some weeks after the first miscarriage, the truck had arrived, and to her surprise, in addition to their orders, there had been a large clay pot containing a rose bush. The rose had been ruby red and heavily scented. Dusty had quietly included it in the order.

He did the same thing after the next two miscarriages.

The rose bushes had outgrown their pots, and he had dug a deep garden bed, enriching the soil from the big compost heap out the back. He had carefully transplanted the roses, and they had both clasped hands and prayed that the roses would not mind the transfer.

They hadn't!

The old woman gets up and leans on the verandah railing, inhaling deeply.

Each rose bush is a different color. The first is the ruby red; the second has roses of bright yellow and the third, roses of soft pink.

The old lady sighs and settles back into her rocker again.

As the years have passed, she's lost contact with the rest of the world.

She and Dusty had lived a solitary life. However, it had become even lonelier after Dusty had gone.

Sitting in her chair, she looks down at the book on the little rickety cane table beside her. The pages are tissue-thin, the cover frayed and worn.

Her mother had given her the old Bible on her wedding day. It had belonged to her great-great-grandmother.

Apparently, after the *Change*, her great-great-grandfather had gone away with someone called *Traveler*, to seek out other copies, if they existed.

They found them of course, and the precious books had been taken back to the people in the mountain community, who'd been keenly waiting for them.

(She amazes herself at how some of her mother's stories can pop back up with startling clarity.)

She had never really bothered with the old Bible at first, but then she had begun to read it.

The words had sung to her.

Every day she would settle into her rocker, open the worn, frayed cover and let the music in its pages bring warmth and comfort to her heart, especially when Dusty was away.

As time passed, she developed a relationship with the main character of the book, sharing her heart and thoughts with him, asking him about the things she read, talking to him about anything and everything.

She sighs and softly tries to sing a few lines from an old hymn she knew as a child. Her voice doesn't have the strength it once did, and it breaks before she gets to the end of the first chorus.

"Broken down old voice," she croaks. "Just as well there is nobody around to hear me."

Her thoughts return to Dusty.

She never went out riding with Dusty, as he hadn't wanted her getting involved in *his* work. He called her his *Desert Rose* and said that he didn't want her ending up burnt brown by the sun or smelling of horses and cattle. He'd been such a romantic.

She had missed him terribly every time he rode off to tend to this or that, and she would count the days and the hours until she saw him riding back along the track toward the house.

He would walk his horse across the yard, whistling their tune and she would fly out through the door, her arms open. She'd cover his face with kisses, and they'd both fall about laughing, at the dirt which transferred from him to her.

They would wander hand in hand to the bathhouse behind the house, discarding boots and clothes along the way.

Standing under the overhead drum, Dusty would pull on the rope, sending cool water sluicing over them.

After that they would run into the house, dripping water. Dusty would toss her onto the iron-framed bed and wrap her up in the beautiful cotton rose-patterned bedspread, kissing her and telling her how much he had missed her.

When he was home, he loved her. Oh! How he loved her.

Now and then he would order something pretty from a catalog. One time it was a lovely dinner set; white with tiny pink rosebuds all over it. She had wept as they unpacked the beautiful set together.

Another time, it was a long gown called a Kimono. She had gasped when she saw the beautiful peacock colors and felt the smooth, cool fabric. He had made her put it on and told her that the rich greens matched her eyes. Dusty had set a record on the old phonograph, and as the lovely waltz played, he had taken her in his arms and whirled her around the room. The blue and green Kimono had floated about her like wings, and her long dark hair had fanned out, loose and free, just the way he loved it.

A tear trickles down her wrinkled cheek.

She would give anything, to have her Dusty with her again and hear him whistling their tune.

Some nights, as she lies alone in the big old bed, the scent of the Gumtrees wafting in through the window, she turns her face toward his empty pillow and can't help crying.

She is on her own. Old, tired, alone with her memories, the creak of the windmill and the sounds of the desert.

CHAPTER 35

Heartache and Loss

The sun is casting long shadows across the ground, and the desert breeze now holds a chill.

The old woman rubs her arms. She is feeling the cold a lot more these days, not to mention being tired. Oh, so tired.

Easing herself out of the rocker, she limps on stiff legs back into the house. Time to put the kettle on. A hot cup of tea will help warm her up.

Some time later, as she sits in the sagging old armchair by the firebox, her memories pick up the thread of her parents.

They are long gone, having died in a car accident, shortly after she and Dusty married and moved to the property. She had been left with a sizeable inheritance from the sale of their house and business.

Dusty's parents had died some years later, and Dusty had inherited the huge property and everything that came with it. However, he had not wanted to live in the parent's big homestead. He'd had the property subdivided, and a portion of it sold off, along with the dark furnishings and chattels from the big old house.

The funds from all of these events and their cattle sales had continued to sit in the bank accumulating interest.

Living the simple life, they had not needed much. Material goods had not interested them. They had just loved life itself and being together. The bank had taken care of everything else and still did.

What had happened to Dusty?

She doesn't know.

Some of the land's *custodians*, (that's what Dusty had called the dark-skinned people) had stopped at the house briefly one morning. They'd been passing through on a long *walkabout*.

Dusty had spoken with them for a while before they disappeared down the track, heading to goodness knows where.

Dusty had told her they'd spotted a break in the fence and a few strays had been seen wandering out in the desert. He said it sounded like it was in the furthermost top end of the property. Dusty had made the decision to head off and investigate.

He had put his kit together, taken his favorite rifle and headed off. She remembered his wave as he turned in his saddle, yelling out: "See you soon, *Desert Rose*. I'll be back by Christmas."

He always used to say that. It was a joke between them.

She'd stood on the verandah, listening to him whistling their tune as he disappeared down the track, fading into the haze and heat shimmer.

After two weeks had passed, she'd made inquiries through the radiotelephone, asking if anyone had seen him. She thought he might have stopped off somewhere.

No-one had seen him.

She had waited.

After four weeks had gone by with no sign of him and no word, efforts were made to look for him. Resources had been limited, and due to the vastness of the property and the landscape, it had been like looking for a needle in a haystack.

Months had passed by. Hope had dwindled.

As time passed, she had faced the unavoidable truth that she was now on her own. Dusty would not be coming home.

Grief made its permanent home in her heart.

The old woman leans back and closes her eyes.

A gentle breeze stirs the fine tendrils of silver framing her wrinkled face.

Laugh lines have deepened into lines of sorrow.

Eyes that once danced and sparkled have become resigned in their expression.

Roses and red bull dust fill her vision. Longing and loneliness fill her heart.

CHAPTER 36

'Josh' arrives.

One afternoon as she sits on the verandah, the old woman sees something. She leans forward.

A man appears, walking out of the shimmering heat haze. She strains to see him more clearly.

Why on earth would anyone be wandering the desert on their own? He doesn't have a horse and as far as she can tell there is no truck or vehicle beyond him. Perhaps it has broken down some way back along the track?

The man draws closer and is soon standing in front of the house. He is fairly tall, ordinary looking, with clothes that are patched and dirty. He wears a stained, wide-brimmed hat on his head. On his back, he carries a rolled up swag, from which Billy-cans and odds and ends are dangling.

The stranger takes off his scruffy hat and calls out a polite greeting.

To see someone walk up to the house is a shock. Her only visitors on foot are the *custodians* of the land, and she can't even remember the last time they passed through.

"Ma'am?" the man queries, leaning forward slightly, his hat held across his chest.

She gives a start. She has been drifting again. It happens a lot these days.

"I'm sorry! I was daydreaming. Hello, my name is Ruth. And yours?"

"You can call me *Josh*."

She thinks his answer a bit odd, but she lets it slide.

Curious, she asks him where he comes from.

"From all over! Today, I am here. Do you have any work I can do?"

The old woman thinks for a minute.

"Well, some things do need fixing. I can't pay you money, but are a camp-bed and food okay?"

He smiles, assuring her that that is all he needs.

Josh politely asks for a drink.

Ruth clucks her tongue.

"Where are my manners? I'll get you something."

She points him to the tap beneath the water tank so he can freshen up. While he does that, she fetches a jug of homemade lemonade and a plate of biscuits.

Ruth is dumbfounded.

How has he made it this far out?

As a child she heard tales of people wandering lost for days, only to end up dying of thirst and exposure.

She shakes her head as she carries out the tray.

Ruth's visitor sits on the verandah steps, his back against the railing. He drains a glass of the cooling drink and helps himself to a couple of the biscuits.

"You're very kind to give me a welcome, Ruth. Many would turn me away in an instant."

She can't understand why. It is an unspoken rule of the Outback that you help others. It isn't so much about doing a good turn; it is a matter of survival. The day might come when you need a helping hand yourself.

Having had nobody to speak to face to face for a very long time, she wants to hear him talk.

"Josh, would you mind telling me about your travels, people you've met, things you've seen? I just want to listen."

He nods, knowing the aching loneliness in her, understanding her need.

He shares with her about the happenings in other parts of the country and tells her how some country towns have grown, while others are dying due to drought conditions. He describes in detail, the hustle and bustle of crowded cities.

She laughs when he tells her that one day men will be walking on the moon.

Time passes, and he sees that she is weary.

"I'll stop now, Ruth. I'd like to stay a while and be of help to you. You don't have to do anything for me. I can look after myself."

Ruth thanks him and shows him the stretcher on the verandah where he can sleep and keep his gear.

While he sorts out his bits and pieces, she goes off to put together a simple meal.

When it is over, they clean up together, before each heads off to sleep.

As Ruth dreams of old time dances, blue eyes, and a cheeky smiling face, her visitor stands on the verandah gazing up at the star-filled expanse overhead...black velvet covered in sparkling diamonds that wink and twinkle. The moon paints the desert landscape in her entrancing, silver light.

Stepping off the verandah, he paces slowly around the buildings. He doesn't need a lamp to see because night is as day to him.

The ramshackle sheds have fallen into a state of disrepair. Some are overgrown with wild creepers, and some are sagging like a tired, worn-out clothesline.

He stands under the huge old Gumtree, gazing down at the three small crosses. Her efforts to keep the weeds at bay are proving unsuccessful. He pulls at them, disturbing a brown snake which slithers away quickly.

The man called *Josh* continues walking around the property, keeping near to the house. As he walks, he sings softly, the notes drifting, sparkling...trailing behind him like a cloak...a cloak of lights and shadows.

CHAPTER 37

A Time for Weeping

Over the next few days, Ruth watches her new friend pulling down gnarled vines and digging out weeds. He is always humming or singing as he works.

Ruth marvels that Josh never seems to grow tired, no matter how hard the physical work is. He comes to the verandah at the end of the day, looking as fresh as when he started, albeit covered in dust and dirt.

She puts it down to his younger years. Although she has to admit, it's hard to tell how old he is.

Ruth likes having him around. She wonders where he's come from and if he has family anywhere.

A few days later they are both sitting on the verandah enjoying mugs of tea.

"Josh, do you have any family?"

"Oh, I have family everywhere," he replies, smiling.

"But where were you born?" she asks.

"In a little town a long way from here. Your turn now, Ruth. Tell me why you are out here on your own."

At this, Ruth goes still.

He sees the pain in her face and quietly waits.

"I don't know why I am on my own. My husband and I were very close. Being a cattle property, he often needed to go out checking fences and the stock. Sometimes he'd be away for days, but he always came home, always!"

Ruth looks down at the mug of tea in her hands.

"One day there was something he had to do in a far corner of the property. I remember waving him goodbye. That was the last I saw of him."

She gazes out, her eyes unfocused.

He waits.

When she resumes, her voice is trembling.

"He used to hum and whistle a little tune all the time. I never knew what it was. I never thought to ask. How strange. It was a lovely little song. It was the first thing I heard when I started at the small country school. (She sighs deeply.) It was the last thing I heard as he rode away."

Her voice breaks and she sobs, holding her apron over her face. After a few moments, she catches her breath.

"I'm so sorry, Josh. I'm just a silly old woman. Please forgive me."

He goes over and puts his arms around her.

At his touch, she stiffens, but then the dam bursts and she collapses into his arms. It is the first time she has received a comforting embrace. Her frail little body shakes as the heavy burden of her loss pours out.

He holds her close, letting her sorrow pour out upon him.

When her sobs have subsided, she wipes her face on her apron and smiles tremulously.

"Thank you, Josh. I think that has been a long time in coming."

Getting up slowly she pats her hair.

"I must look a sight. I'm sorry I fell apart on you. I'll get some more tea."

He returns to his seat on the steps, groaning deeply within himself. No soul should ever *apologize* for weeping. How could grief and weeping offend him? Weeping is a language all on its own. It is a language which expresses great joy or great pain in the soul.

The man called *Josh* thinks of another woman who wept. Her name was *Mary*. She had walked into a room filled with critical, self-righteous men and openly poured her heart out upon him. Her weeping had offended those around them. However, her tears had been an *anointing* upon him, for they were the outpouring of her soul. He had rebuked the men for their hard-heartedness.

No, he does not despise the weeping of the heart, nor will he ever turn away from those who pour their grief and sorrow upon him.

While he stands on the verandah gazing up at the heavens, a shadow blots out the stars.

A great bird sweeps down, its mighty wings beating the air as it comes to rest on the old verandah railing, which creaks and sways slightly beneath the bird's weight.

"Hello, my friend. I was wondering when you would show up."

He strokes the beautiful feathers, and the eagle dips its head, making soft sounds deep in its throat.

"Yes, I know what happened."

The eagle cocks its head, fixing a keen yellow eye on its companion's face.

Ruth's husband had made the long trek to the far border of the vast property. He had rounded up the strays and herded them back through the gap in the fence-line. Once they were safely in, he had tethered his horse to a nearby tree, before turning to work on the fence. After he had completed the repairs, he had walked his horse through the long grass to a waterhole which was some distance away.

The waterhole was at the base of a mass of gigantic boulders and rocky outcrops.

As the man and his horse had drawn close to the waterhole, a large boar had suddenly rushed out from among the reeds. It had ugly curved tusks and was a mighty beast.

The horse had panicked, ripping the reins out of the man's hands. It turned to bolt, but as it did, it got tangled up in the dangling reins, the reeds, and its own feet. The horse went crashing down.

The huge boar had ripped into the fallen horse's belly without a moment's hesitation.

The horse, out of its mind with pain, had struggled to its feet, slipping in its blood and intestines. Its shrill screams and the smell of hot blood had sent the huge boar into an even greater frenzy. It wasn't long before the poor horse was dead.

The man had tried to get out of the way of the carnage by clambering up the high boulders and rocks. In his hasty climb, he had slipped, falling into a deep crevasse between two of the enormous boulders. His fall had ended on a jagged branch. Impaled and unable to move, the man had known death was imminent. With tears flowing down his face, he had begun humming a little tune until, unable to continue, he lapsed into silence. "Ruth" was the last sound he breathed.

CHAPTER 38

Homecoming

One day, to Ruth's surprise, she hears a rumbling noise coming from along the track. She calls Josh, and together they stand on the verandah, watching and waiting.

They see it is a truck.

Josh gently puts his arm around Ruth's frail shoulders. He knows what the truck is carrying.

The truck comes to a halt in a billowing red cloud. The driver jumps out and approaches the steps.

"Hi Ruth, it's been a long time since we've done this run. How are you faring?"

"I'm doing well. This is my handyman, Josh. He's been helping me and doing an excellent job. What brings you out here? Come in and have a cup of tea."

The driver looks down, shuffling his feet. He puts his hands in his pockets then pulls them out again. He doesn't seem to know what to do with them.

"I'll just have a cold drink, please Ruth, and a couple of biscuits if you have any."

The two men wait while Ruth goes into the house, emerging a few minutes later with drinks and biscuits. After he finishes his drink, the driver's voice takes on a more serious tone.

"Ruth, some prospectors were working in an area beyond the far northern end of your property. They found something and took it with them when they returned to the nearest town. It was sent on to us, and I've brought it out here to you."

He indicates the back of the truck with a nod of his head.

She looks over. There is a tarpaulin tied down and something under it.

"What is it?" she asks, curious.

"I think you should come and see, Ruth. Can you walk with her?" he asks Josh.

They help Ruth down from the verandah and approach the tray of the truck. The driver undoes the holding straps at one corner and pulls the tarpaulin back, revealing the remains of a saddle and an old rifle.

Ruth looks at them, uncomprehending at first.

"I'm so sorry Ruth," the driver says. "The prospectors found a few bones scattered about, *horse* bones (he said hurriedly) and amazingly, this was found nearby. It's pretty chewed up and ruined; been out there for many long years. The rifle is way beyond useless as well."

"Are you telling me they belonged to Dusty?" she whispers, clutching his arm.

"You can still see his markings and name on both," the truck driver replies softly.

The driver feels terrible. This isn't the sort of thing he likes to deliver. Not to someone like this lovely old woman who has been stuck out here for decades, wondering why her husband never came home.

Ruth draws closer to the saddle and the rifle. She touches them with shaking fingers.

"There were no...(she hesitates)...signs of Dusty?"

"Oh Ruth, I wish I could tell you that there weren't. The prospectors had been investigating an old crevasse, a deep one and while doing so...they found the remains of a man.

The bones had not been touched by any wildlife. The hole was too deep."

The driver looks at Josh, and his eyes are full of pain.

Ruth sees the deep sorrow on his face, and her hands clutch at her apron.

"There was an old leather belt, still intact and, I'm sorry Ruth, but Dusty's name was still visible. He'd etched it into the leather when he made it. I remember him showing it to me on one of my runs out here."

The driver looks at Josh, who nods. He knows what is coming.

"Ruth...I've brought Dusty home."

Ruth hears the driver's words but is having difficulty comprehending them.

Dusty has been found? Her Dusty?

As understanding comes, she sinks to the ground.

Josh holds onto her, and they sit together in the dust. She rocks back and forth, hands over her face, keening softly, her tears falling onto the arms of the one who is holding her.

The men wait quietly, respecting her grief.

When Ruth feels strong enough, the two men help her up and escort her back to her rocker.

She pats Josh's hand.

"I'll be alright. It's just the shock. After all these years of not knowing. Poor Dusty."

The driver explains that Dusty's remains have been placed in a coffin. As she quietly watches, they unload the coffin and the other items, putting them on the verandah.

Josh goes in to make some tea.

It is a quiet trio who sit on the verandah, staring out at the beautiful landscape, each in their thoughts.

When the two men have finished, they slip out back to the huge Gumtree, to prepare a place for Dusty's remains.

Ruth sips her tea slowly.

Her Dusty is finally home.

He is with her again.

Warmed by the tea, she lets herself slip into a peaceful haze. A strange warmth envelops her heart.

Josh has quietly returned to the corner of the old house from where he watches her. He hums softly under his breath. The gentle tune wraps itself around her, like a soft, warm blanket.

Chapter 39

Songs in the Sunset

Ruth is smiling. Today she will put Dusty under the huge old Gumtree, next to his three little ones.

The sun shines warmly. A soft breeze sighs in through the open windows, stirring the gauzy curtains and the faded drapes; their patterns almost invisible due to age, sunlight, and washing.

Together Ruth and the two men place the coffin, saddle, and rifle in the grave. Ruth prays a prayer and says her final goodbye.

The truck driver makes his farewells.

"I'm sorry Ruth. I have to get going. I'm glad you have your handyman here. Please use your radio if you need to contact somebody in the town or if you need something brought out. I'm so very sorry Ruth."

She smiles and thanks the driver for his kindness.

While she waves goodbye, the truck departs in a cloud of billowing dust.

The rest of the day passes quietly.

Not much is said.

Ruth has a gentle smile on her face throughout.

They are sitting on the verandah as the sun is sinking.

Ruth loves this time of the day.

She peers at the roses.

"Oh look Josh. The roses are wilting."

She sighs.

"They've bloomed beautifully, but now their time is coming to an end."

Josh looks over at her with tenderness on his face.

"Yes, Ruth...bloomed beautifully, but now coming to an end."

As the final rays of the sun paint the desert and front of the house red-gold, Ruth suddenly clutches his arm.

"I'm afraid Josh. Why am I afraid?"

He takes her hands in his.

"There's no need to be afraid Ruth. *Look* at me."

She turns her head, looking into his face.

There is something different.

His face is shining with so much love that it takes her breath away. She sees what appears to be a glow shimmering in the air all around him. *But isn't that just the light of the sunset?*

"Who are you Josh?" she whispers, her small wrinkled hands gripping his.

"Don't you know me, Ruth? You hear my music in the pages of the old Bible."

His voice is extraordinarily tender.

"We've been friends for a long time."

She stares at him for some moments, then wonder fills her face, as the Wonder of who he is, floods her heart.

A sound catches her ears, and she turns her head.

A man is crossing the yard, walking through the flaring red rays of sunset. He is leading a horse, and he is whistling *their* tune.

185

As the very last ray of the setting sun paints the landscape in a warm, golden glow, a young woman with long dark hair and flowing kimono, runs with arms outstretched, toward the young man crossing the yard. She flings herself into his embrace, and he swings her around, her long dark hair fanning out and the beautiful kimono spreading like wings behind her. For a moment they both sparkle then, as the sun slips below the horizon, soft singing and a cloak of lights and shadows enfold them...and they fade away.

Epilogue

The truck driver has forgotten his clipboard. Thankfully he's not that far along the track.

He hits the brakes and comes to a halt in a cloud of dust. Grinding the old gears, he turns the truck around and heads back to the little homestead, keeping a watch out for kangaroos. It's twilight. The time when they're usually out and about.

After pulling into the yard, he gets out and looks around for the man Josh. There is no sign of him.

The little house sits in darkness.

"Surely they can't have gone somewhere," he thinks to himself.

It is when he mounts the steps of the verandah that he sees the old woman's shape, slumped in the rocking chair.

"Oh no! Ruth!"

The truck driver hastily goes to her. However, he knows she has gone.

He kneels down beside the chair and stares at her. On her face, there is a look of joy as if she'd seen something wonderful in her last moments.

Tears well up in the driver's eyes.

She was a dear little thing. So brave to keep living out here on her own.

He gently eases the old Bible out from under her hands and puts it aside.

There is no question of his driving back now. He will do what he can before radioing for someone to come out.

He wonders what will happen to the little homestead and the collection of memories within.

After cranking up the old generator (which amazingly still has fuel in it), the driver lays Ruth down on the bed and wraps her in the cotton bedspread, the one with the faded rose pattern. He knows she loved her roses.

The man Josh still hasn't made an appearance so the driver concludes that he must have left, although why he would just up and leave the old woman, is beyond him.

Sitting by the wood-stove, the driver casually picks up the old Bible. Ruth had always talked about how much she loved it. She used to say that it *sang* to her.

Curious, he opens it.

Something falls out onto the floor.

He sees that it is an embroidered bookmark. As he puts it back in place, his eye is caught by an underlined verse.

'The LORD thy God, in the midst of thee, is mighty; he will save, he will rejoice over thee with joy; he will rest in his love, he will joy over thee with singing.'[12]

Two hours later, David Stalwart is still reading.

About the Author

Hailing originally from New Zealand, Jan immigrated to Australia in the early 1980's. She lives with her husband Peter, and fearless feline KoKo, in the beautiful Granite Belt of South East Queensland. Jan has three married children and six grandchildren. She is an experienced writer, a talented artist, and a trained classical pianist. Jan loves life, her family, and friends. She has a deep abiding faith in God and believes that real, healthy laughter can cure just about anything.

Contact details: janmau@maucasso.com
Website: www.maucasso.com

Endnotes

[1] Psalm 30 verse 5b. New Schofield Reference Bible, 1967 Edition. (All scriptures quoted, are from the NSRB, 1967 Edition.)

[2] Catawba is a shade of red, similar to Grape. Catawba has the hex (RGB) value #703642 on A-Z lists of colors and their variations.

[3] *Trauermarsch* is German for 'Funeral March': a musical composition.

[4] Scientists now have a way of hearing the sounds made by nebulas, stars and other celestial bodies. I Googled "stars singing" and found a plethora of sites and information on this subject. Many provide links where you can listen to these amazing sounds.

[5] Psalm 149 v 3

[6] Psalm 149 v 4, 5

[7] Exodus 20 v 13

[8] Exodus 20 v 1a

[9] John 3 v 16

[10] Isaiah 61 v 1

[11] John 3 v 8

[12] Zephaniah 3 v 17

Printed in the United States
By Bookmasters